UNDER THE CURSE

UNDER THE CURSE

JacQueline Vaughn Roe

To Justin, Sarah, and Grace,

I have many favorite readers,
but the three of you encourage me
with your notes of impatience.

Here is Under the Curse,
and I'll try to write Among the Kingdoms faster.

May you continue to love the journey God has you on!

RONA
Queen's Tower
King Purnell's Castle
Lord Colin
Sir Reginald
Castle of Silver Birds
Maer
Kabir Island
Illyan Sea
N
E
S
W

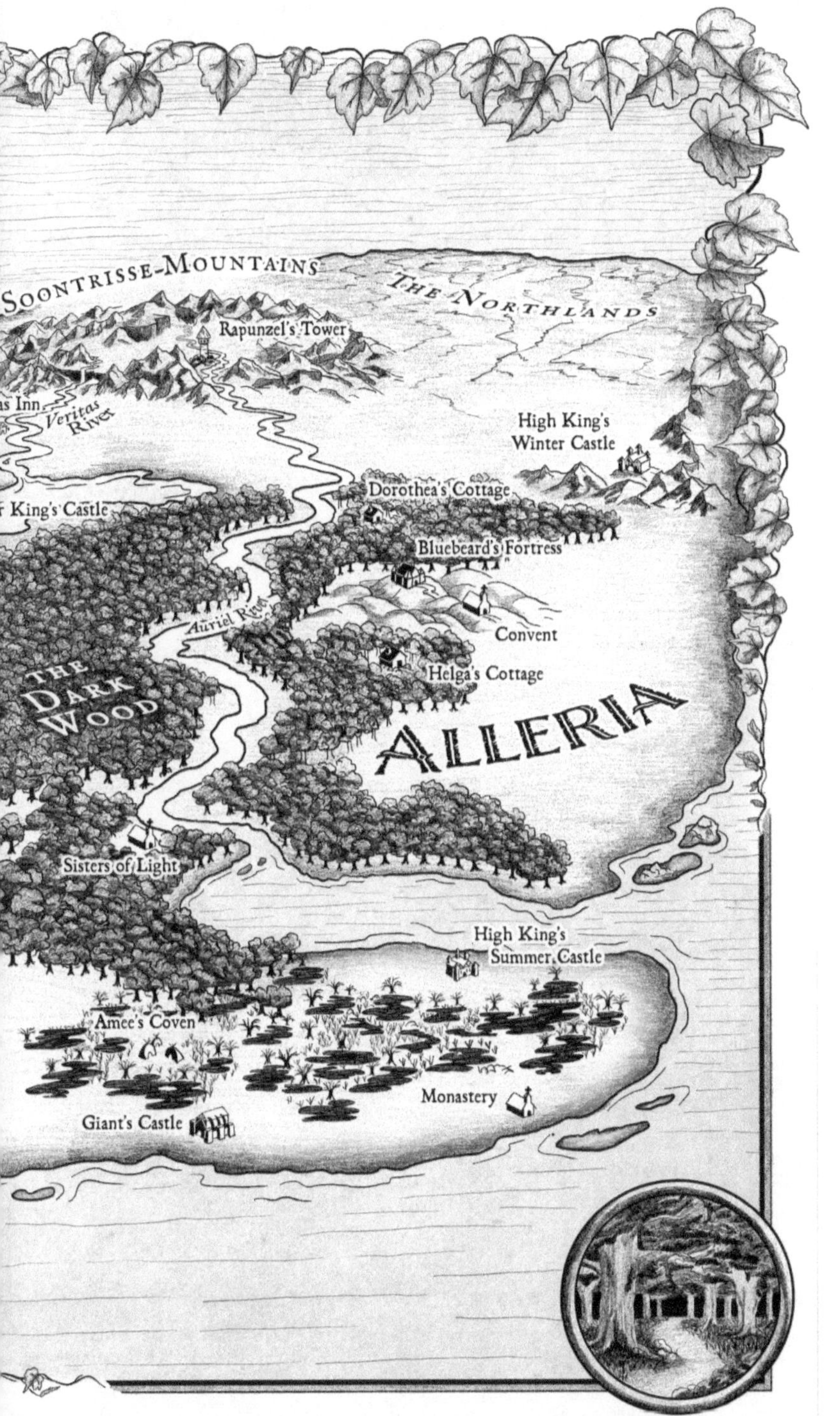

Soontrisse Mountains
The Northlands
Rapunzel's Tower
...as Inn
Veritas River
High King's Winter Castle
...r King's Castle
Dorothea's Cottage
Bluebeard's Fortress
Auriel River
Convent
THE DARK WOOD
Helga's Cottage
ALLERIA
Sisters of Light
High King's Summer Castle
Amee's Coven
Monastery
Giant's Castle

CONTENTS

PROLOGUE

The shock jolted the sisters awake. Across time and space they could see one another in their human forms, floating above a black lake lit by a green light deep within its heart. They were under the mountain, in the eldest sister's lair, surrounded by sharp walls of a cavern. Ute, her white hair flowing around her levitating form, was shaking with laughter. Black eyes flashed as she raised her long pale arms in triumph. "She is coming to me, sisters, and soon we will reunite. The power will be ours! Are you ready?"

Camilla blinked her grey eyes slowly and licked her full red lips. Was it finally time? She had been waiting for nearly thirty years, having placed the small human on the road to empowering her. For years, she had despaired over losing the prince when she could no longer track him. But then, last spring and throughout the summer, he had returned to her domain, bringing such outpourings of power that she could now roam on shore. Her followers were growing stronger, and her boundaries were decreasing bit by bit. It would happen! She could see her sisters in person again. They would use their powers to free the people from the tyranny of the weak god they served mindlessly.

Amee jerked her head upright, dark eyes showing almost no whites, reminding Camilla of the centaur her sister shifted into. Little sister, always the favorite, Camilla couldn't help doting on her. They called her *ah-may* because she had come in the spring, the long-awaited child after Ute and Camilla were grown. She couldn't think of her any other way besides being a little sister, even though Camilla had witnessed her sister's cunning and strength during the war. That had been before Amee had allowed one weakness into her life. Camilla could not dwell on that now. Her little sister had made, and would continue to make, amends.

Amee spoke with authority, her alto voice echoing off the jagged walls. "My covens are ready. When will it be?"

The sound of babes crying filled the air, and Ute laughed in glee. "She has arrived, I must go to her. Begin the stirring, sisters, and she will join us. The power will enter you before dawn and free us at last."

Camilla nodded across the expanse toward Amee who raised her hands to swirl the waters into a whipping froth. "You look well."

Amee looked up with unblinking eyes, her concentration momentarily suspended. "I have missed you, Camilla. I thought, when we separated, that you and I could still meet at the edge of the marsh. Why can't we?"

"There was a barrier that prevented me from reaching the western shores of the Northlands and Alleria. But the curse has weakened slightly and I can now go there, but not beyond. I cannot even approach the Eastern Ports."

Amee nodded her head in resignation.

Camilla lifted her hands in response and smiled as she spoke into the green glow that pulsed from the waters below.

"But it is all about to change. Are you prepared to make your ultimate sacrifice?"

Did her sister hesitate? Camilla frowned when Amee's dark eyes dropped for a moment. "I thought what I'd already given would be enough."

Sacrifices could be hard. It was the nature of such things. Her sister needed more resolve so her weakness could become her strength. "It might be, but are you willing to do what we must do?"

Amee gave a clipped nod.

"Good. We will see it through, all of us. The babes will die, Rapunzel will join us, and that will be enough. We will be together and it will all be worth it."

Silence descended as the sisters meditated on their tasks. Camilla pulled from the depths of the sea the icy darkness to swirl together with the heat of Amee's marsh. Together they stirred the elements in with the frozen peaks of the Northlands. In guttural tones they moaned the names of the lost children they had used to restore their power.

Lightning struck from high above, and currents of electricity danced across the swirling waters. They could hear Ute calling out, and her form appeared before them. Two little ones, one toddler and one babe, rotated in the air with Rapunzel, their faces grotesque masks of pain as Ute pulled their hearts from their chests. Camilla felt her smile split, and a laugh filled the air until the young woman cried out, "Jesu! Save me!"

The portal closed, her sisters vanished, and the dark depths of water surrounded Camilla instantly. "No!" she screamed, her words floating up in bubbles. "No! No!" She reached forward to find the portal again, pulled from the strength she had harnessed just a moment ago. Gone! She had no access. Her form shifted into a long, eel-like leviathan so she could breathe, her tentacles wrapped close to her sides. Her tail pushed behind her and she flew upward, breaking the surface of the sea above. She dove back down below, spinning faster and faster into the depths, raging and crying at her loss. Where did they go? How would she ever find her way back to them?

A HARSH AWAKENING

The words were barely out of Prince Edmund's mouth when Gwynndolen's fist collided with his jaw. He hadn't expected her to hit so hard. In truth, he hadn't expected her to hit him at all.

She struck him again, and he stumbled backward in shock while her brothers snickered. "Shut your mouths!" she commanded, and one by one, they stopped, suddenly more interested in their weapons of choice. "How dare you?" she spat at Edmund, and he wondered if her fury would turn her eyes as red as her hair.

"I meant nothing by it." His breath was visible in the chilly spring air, and he tenderly touched his jaw which ached to the roots of his teeth.

"I never took you for a liar, Your Highness."

"Gwynndolen, you can't say—" her brother Georgius began, but she cut him off.

"I'll speak the truth to whoever needs to hear it! The prince needs to hear it." She fumed at Edmund: "Rapunzel left you and she's gone, it's true, but that doesn't make her less for not choosing Your Highness. If you were a better man, I would think you would wish her well—especially since she had to escape a witch to find her love."

At this, her brothers chortled but stopped at the flash of her eyes as she turned once more to them. "You men, what do you know of love?" She turned back to the prince and pierced his very core. "Was she really who you wanted, or were you just *making* her what you wanted?" She stepped over to her stallion and mounted, leaving Edmund behind in dumb silence.

Only when she was safely out of hearing distance did Georgius laugh aloud, and his brother joined in. Georgius sheathed his sword and walked over to Edmund, clapping the prince on his shoulder and then roughing his sandy hair with a massive paw. "Don't mind Gwynndolen. She's a bit much at times, but she's also the best horsewoman I know. She'll cool down and still be able to help you later."

The prince wasn't sure how he felt about that. The lady had looked ready to kill him. He had noticed that she and Rapunzel had become close the summer before, but he didn't realize a careless word would cause her to attack him. The brothers shrugged off the incident and surrounded him again with their weapons raised. He rotated his sword in anticipation and returned to practice instead of going for a riding lesson. Each parry, advance, and dodge made his body sore enough that he no longer took much notice of his jaw. Not much.

⚬⚬⚬

GWYNNDOLEN COULD HEAR her horse's labored breathing. Trees had been flying past her, pale green leaves a blur as she tried to escape her own fury. Her grip loosened as she tried to ease off. Her powerful stallion wasn't frothing at the mouth, but he would be if she kept pushing. Where was she, anyway?

Gently, she pulled on the reins, and her horse slowed to a walk. She was at the edge of the wood which spread for miles behind the castle. How had she come so far without realizing it? It was ridiculous that she could let that—that *prince* unsettle her so! Lady Genevieve, her adoptive mother, had often warned her of her temper, told her repeatedly it would get her in trouble, but she hadn't listened.

Gwynndolen sighed and turned the stallion around to head back through the wood. It was still early, but there was no reason she couldn't spend the rest of the day cleaning out the stables and checking on the horses. Hard labor would help her calm down, she knew from experience. She hoped the stable hands here at Lord Col's estate wouldn't mind. She had planned on spending most of the morning with the prince once he finished his lessons with her brothers, but that seemed unlikely now.

Even if Prince Edmund was horrid, she needed to remember her place. He would one day be her sovereign. While her family enjoyed good relations with his father, the king, that was no guarantee Edmund would get along with her. He could see that she didn't marry—never did well at court.

The thought put a smirk on her impish face, and her dark Ronan eyes glittered with mischief. Gwynndolen clicked her tongue and nudged with her heels, picking up the pace a bit. She didn't really care if he did. Perhaps marrying well was all a woman should do, but—maybe it was in her blood? —she'd rather be mucking out a stable. In fact, she was proud of running the stables for her adoptive father on their own estate, and she hoped she would continue to do so far into the future.

No, she would leave the worries of courtly life to her sister, Beatrix, who still thought she could turn the prince's head now that Rapunzel had left Rona for the Northlands. Was it wrong that she hoped her sister would marry at the High King's court this summer and not return home with their family? Better yet, Beatrix could marry the prince and they could live together; they might deserve each other. It would be difficult enough to be around them through the coming season, but if by the end, it could rid her of her conniving sister . . .

Gwynndolen sighed. "Queen Beatrix" was a daunting idea. Perhaps not even Prince Edmund deserved such a woman.

◌◦⁂◦◌

RAPUNZEL SAT up like an arrow sprung from its bow. "What's wrong?" Paul murmured, peeking open his eyes, but only seeing the dim outline of his wife's moving form in the darkness.

"I thought I heard something."

"You didn't hear anything. The baby is fine, go back to sleep."

"I will, but—"

"Rapunzel, she's fine. Let the servant handle things tonight. It's Jehanne, she knows how to care for Helena. Allow her to do her duty and we can get one night of sleep —" He reached through the darkness for her, but she was too quick.

"I'll be back in a moment, my love." She slipped from beneath the sheets and padded away toward Helena's room, shutting the door softly behind her.

Paul grunted and stretched. It wouldn't be long; it was the same game every night. Soon the door creaked open with the sound of his wife's steps coming closer. She pushed the babe toward him, saying, "Hold her while I climb in, please."

He didn't argue, but reached out and pulled the baby up close to him. "Why are you awake, little one? You should be sleeping." The babe, who would soon be toddling, giggled at his voice and swiped at him with a moist hand she had been sucking on. "She seems fine to me, Rapunzel."

"Oh, you didn't hear her when I went into her room. She was so sad. Jehanne was having trouble getting her to settle down after her milk and—Paul, she needed me."

"She needs to sleep."

"She can sleep with us."

"She needs to sleep in her own room. You know Jehanne can—"

"No, she can't. Jehanne doesn't know her like I do. God entrusted her to me—he allowed me to rescue her from Ute. I need to be the one taking care of her. I told Jehanne to go back to bed, that we wouldn't be needing her anymore tonight."

Or ever, Paul thought as he sighed. He knew Rapunzel would have her way in the end, but he frowned into the darkness. It wouldn't be this way forever. He shifted to make room to tuck Rapunzel into his side as she tucked Helena into hers. The babe made chattering sounds and he ached. He had grown to love holding his wife and his child this way. But no, she wasn't his. She wasn't Rapunzel's. How hard it would be when it was time to return Helena to her family. Would his wife be able to let go? Would he?

Acting like parents so soon after marrying had been strange. The fact that the child had been imprisoned from infancy by Ute, drained of her lifeblood to supply the sorceress with power, complicated it. She had been sickly when they rescued her at the onset of winter, and was only now, in the spring thaw, starting to develop into the chubby, happy baby girl she should have been all along.

He wondered what the child would remember about the wrong done to her. Rapunzel's rushing to Helena each night had come from the child waking up screaming and his wife being the only one who could soothe her. Perhaps her experiences in Ute's cavernous castle were still clinging to the child. It seemed right that Rapunzel, once imprisoned in a tower by a witch, should rescue such a one and bring her home.

When the babe refused to nurse, Katterina, Rapunzel's mother, had helped them fashion a vessel from a ram's horn and a leather pouch for feeding the little one fresh goat's milk. Princesses in the Northlands traditionally gave over the care of their babies to a servant, but Rapunzel seemed incapable of being traditional. Paul listened as her breathing deepened, and he felt her body relax. They had christened the child shortly after they arrived back in his uncle's castle; it had seemed foolhardy not to. But now, Paul wondered, was all of this going to make it that much harder for them to let her go?

He knew his young wife struggled with the additional responsibilities of court. Was she hiding behind the guise of motherhood? He was trying to learn to be a good father as long as they had the little one, but he wanted to protect his heart, protect his wife's heart. And if his uncle, the Fisher King, had anything to say, there would be more heaped onto them soon. He pulled Rapunzel closer. He didn't want to think of that now. He took in a deep breath and let it out slowly, allowing the cheerful sounds and snuggles of his wife and child lull him back to sleep.

THE WOMAN FROM THE SEA

The sound of the waves lightly splashing to shore soothed Camilla as she raised her head from the waters. The deep darkness where she dwelled caused her to blink in the bright light. She had felt the growing within her, getting stronger since last spring. The power had continued to develop the whole year, now cresting into a fresh spring. Something was happening. Shifting, the power funneled into her and she swam her way to Maer, feeling a pull she recognized instinctively.

There had been a deep loss in the winter, but with that loss came power that flowed through her sleek form. Camilla's leviathan body was black with purple streaks along the tentacles that stretched from her when she needed them. Her form shrank smaller now, pulsing with an electric light that disrupted the darkness below. She knew Ute had died, had sensed it as the portal closed. Camilla had mourned until she realized that her sister's power now hummed inside her— and perhaps inside Amee, too? So much new power for Camilla to feast on, some from Ute and —she stopped the thought and grinned. Camilla had always craved power, but now even more her lust had spread. Her hunger had grown as the power had grown, and she partook of whatever sea creatures appealed to her in a moment. She would steal their strength to supplement her own.

Arriving near the shore of Maer, she felt the change in boundaries again. Her bonds loosened and she could emerge, shifting into her human form, a towering woman with auburn hair. She knew she could not go very far, but to leave the water's edge at all was pure bliss. As she thrust her head above the water and waded to shore, she saw a woman walking at the water's lapping edge. She recognized the woman before her, though Queen Lefwenna was no longer young. The sunlight played on the soft winter-pale skin of the queen, a quiet smile lighting up her delicate features.

Why were the mortals so foolish as to leave Her Majesty alone like this? As she approached, the woman looked up and her face blushed crimson. Camilla looked down at her form. Perhaps it was strange to see a naked woman walk out of the waters. With a little magic, she clothed herself in a translucent gown that reflected the light.

"You've returned," Camilla's voice rasped.

The queen blinked as her lips tightened, refusing to give a response.

"He doesn't know, does he?"

"No—" The mortal queen's words faltered, as though she hated to respond at all.

"I like that you keep me a secret, Your Majesty—it makes things so much more interesting."

"I was forgiven for the ill I've done. Why can't I rid myself of you?"

"Because, silly woman, you made a deal with me. A wish for a wish. Now I must have mine."

"You have had yours. I lost him long ago and only just now got him back."

"Yes, and he is so happy to be back, is he not?"

The queen could not hold her gaze as a tear coursed down her cheek.

"Edmund will make a fine king, as long as he does as I like him to."

Queen Lefwenna's dark eyes flickered back to Camilla. "You must stop."

"Must I? Oh, I doubt that I must."

"Why are you so evil?" Her melodic voice was strained and pitiful to hear. It made Camilla's mouth split into a cruel smile.

"You know why."

"But it was so long ago, and everything is fine now. I thought you would leave us alone."

"You know that I cannot. He used his wish one too many times. If he could just have resisted . . . But he didn't, and now he is mine."

The queen wept openly. "Please, I'll give you anything—everything! Just don't do this!"

Camilla laughed, a throaty cackle that she enjoyed hearing herself. It was so good to be beyond the edge of the sea and up breathing air again. She towered over the slender queen. "Tell him he has an appointment with me tonight." The queen shook her head and moaned, but Camilla retreated to the waters. She could not stay away from them for very long. Not yet. But all that would change soon.

RAPUNZEL SAT on the floor of the humid greenhouse, breathing in the fragrance of the herbs and flowers which blended with the scent of the oilcloth window coverings that sealed in the warmth. This place had become her sanctuary during the cold months of winter. She loved to bring Helena here to play while Paul was hard at work learning the ways of the kingdom or training with his weapons.

She looked with her emerald eyes at the wiggling Helena, and her eyebrows drew close together. Was the babe too small for a baby her age, like the others kept saying? Helena had been so fragile and thin when they first brought her to the castle, but now her arms and legs bunched with delightful rolls of fat. Her round head, which had seemed much too large for her to hold up before, was now supported by a strong, chubby neck. The dull wax-colored hair had fallen out, replaced by wispy black curls. That should count for something. And her eyes—silly Paul kept saying they were violet and not deep blue—were bright with intelligence as she cooed and murmured her baby words. She had begun the hard work of learning to crawl, and Rapunzel laughed as the babe pushed her little bottom in the air and crawled like a bear on all fours. She reached over and patted the little one's bottom. "You're supposed to crawl on your knees, silly!"

"We must get her into something a little shorter if we want her to do that," Katterina said, letting in a cool breath of air when she opened the door to enter the greenhouse.

Rapunzel smiled, brushing a wayward tendril back toward her short, coiled braid. "I hadn't thought about her gown impeding crawling. Oh, what a lot of trouble little ones are!"

Rapunzel's mother lifted her black eyebrows—she had never given into the fashion of plucking them out—her green eyes bright with mischief, as always. "Well, I don't have a great deal of experience in raising little ones myself, since I was Cat during your entire childhood. However, I do remember what the women in our village would dress their crawling babes in. Perhaps I can help make—"

"Mother, when would you have time to do such a thing?

I'm lucky to see you at all these days. You seem to spend most daylight hours with the apothecary and the rest of the time falling asleep in your soup!"

Katterina sat with a huff on the ground, feigning offense. "I only splashed my face in the bowl that one time!"

Rapunzel laughed. It felt good to laugh, to be at ease. The winter had been a soothing balm for their weary bodies. She had always hated the cold season before, but she found her routine in their castle by the shore, healing. She spent her mornings in the greenhouse, gardening and exploring until midday. After eating with Paul and the Fisher King, she would take Helena up to the lighthouse. Watching the waves crash into the white cliffs below, right before naptime, calmed the child as much as it did Rapunzel. She sighed, thinking of how she had spent the afternoons and into the evenings among books, studying the God she had grown to trust and writing their misadventures onto parchment at Paul's encouragement. Yes, it had been a wonderful season.

The winter had given their little family time to recover from the journey that had left them battered once they had conquered the sorceress. They had stopped first in the Soontrisse Mountains to deliver Enguerrand, Paul's nephew, back to his parents. Poor boy, he had, like Helena, been a source of power to fuel Ute. Rapunzel said a quick prayer that he was healing, whenever he came to mind.

While there, Paul's hateful father, King Onfroi, had died. By the time they had paid their respects and returned to the road to complete their journey to the Fisher King's domain, they were weary. Would the weather hold? But God had given them a temporary reprieve to make the last leg of the journey. Rapunzel, Paul, Brother Jacob, her mother, and even their foolish-but-wise jester, Amis, had all suffered broken ribs and worse—but it had been worth it. They had stopped Ute from reuniting the sisters of sorcery, and the kings of the Northlands were set free from the curse that was slowly killing them all. Spring was now awakening the land once more, and they had healed up.

Katterina grabbed Helena when the little one squawked at her own inability to get very far. "How much do you know about this voyage we are to take with the Fisher King?"

Rapunzel lifted a shoulder, reaching for Helena, but Katterina shook her head with a laugh. She blew bubbles into the wee girl's belly, making her giggle. Rapunzel smiled, but her thoughts wandered away. Paul's uncle, the Fisher King, said he was well enough to visit the shore tomorrow after they had broken fast. It was curious; he wanted all of them to join him. She smiled to herself with anticipation. As much as she had enjoyed healing up and finding her footing in the castle this winter, her old restlessness had come back as the snows outside began melting. Paul said she had itchy feet, always wanting to be off. Perhaps the king had something for them to do. Maybe they would go exploring the Fisher King's realm, and that would satisfy her wanderlust, she thought with hope.

THE UNVEILING

Gwynndolen sat squeezed between her sister and the stout Lady Hortensia in the middle of the banquet table in the Great Hall of Maer's castle. Sweat caused her layers of dress to stick to her. The mixed smells of the food which balding Lord Col was serving to everyone as he chattered endlessly made her both hungry and a little nauseated. Not that Gwynndolen hated sizable crowds or the seafood they were eating. Lord Col and Lady Hortensia weren't family she particularly liked, but you can't choose your relatives, especially if you're adopted. And they were nobles, and most nobles acted this way.

Pretense. That was what she really hated.

Gwynndolen despised the outrageous orange-and-turquoise banners running the length of the walls; they hurt her eyes. She detested listening to the latest gossip pouring from Lady Hortensia to the queen concerning the High King and the High Queen's marital issues, now that the kingdoms knew he had taken a mistress and would not give her up. Why did she have to nod along and pretend it was interesting? Or worse, pretend she didn't notice what a spectacle her sister was making of herself.

Beatrix constantly wormed her way into the prince's conversation to riddle him with questions. The only thing that gave Gwynndolen satisfaction was to see how befuddled Prince Edmund was by her sister's attention. She glanced sideways at Beatrix, noticing again that her older sister not only filled out her gowns but made certain that her boat-shaped neckline was much lower on her breasts than Gwynndolen found appropriate. Beatrix, rather brazenly, had even worn the same colors of King Purnell. It was appropriate to defer to the king; though he was their uncle, he was their sovereign. But wearing his colors? Even Beatrix's dark chestnut hair, a much more amiable color than Gwynndolen's fiery red, was loose except for two small braids plaited with ribbons of yellow and black. While Gwynndolen had to admit that Beatrix looked lovely in the bright yellows and dark blacks, it was too forward.

Beatrix flung her yellow tippet in Gwynndolen's face when she reached back for servants to refill her goblet. As Beatrix laughed at her, it reminded Gwynndolen why she hated the long ribbon-like streamers that extended from the elbows of formal gowns. Ridiculous! How could a woman expect to accomplish the most basic things when outfitted in impractical finery?

How Gwynndolen wished she could have made an excuse to eat her meals alone or just with her brothers! But Lady Genevieve had insisted when she sent Gwynndolen to represent their family on the trip that her daughter attend banquets and not occupy her time solely with horses. Gwynndolen knew if she had not agreed, her mother would have kept her home. But what would Lady Genevieve think about the way Beatrix was behaving? Perhaps that's why she insisted Gwynndolen attend banquets and go to court, though Gwynndolen doubted she could ever convince her sister to behave properly.

Beatrix was now twittering. Gwynndolen didn't know what else to call the annoying laugh that her sister had developed when in the prince's presence. She looked away from her sister to the prince sitting across the table, next to the king. His forkful of flaky fish pie froze halfway to his mouth as he stared at the laughing maid. His eyes flitted guiltily over at Gwynndolen, and he put his food down on his trencher and excused himself from the meal. Gwynndolen's aunt, Queen Lefwenna, trailed after him.

Lord Col gave a hearty laugh at the crestfallen Beatrix and said, "Don't worry, lovely maid, there will be other princes when you visit the High King's court this summer. Young, strapping men. Wonderful that he is holding court a year early! What a chance for your generation to make matches, and the traders to make some money, eh?" He laughed boisterously, and the king nodded with a tolerant smile. Gwynndolen knew that Lord Col had not been born of a noble family, but as a rich merchant's son, he had brought sound trading into Rona and saved them from starvation during a drought years past. If this wasn't reason for tolerance, then she really had no idea of what courtly politics were.

A troubadour came into the hall and began singing while strumming his lute, but Gwynndolen wanted to be away. As soon as she could, she exited the hall and made her way outside, thinking to walk around before heading to bed. Coming quickly around a corner, she slammed into the prince and fell onto her backside. "Oof!" she gasped in surprise.

"M-my Lady. Um, I'm sorry." His words stumbled as he tried to help her stand up. "I wasn't watching where I was—"

She felt ashamed at her earlier outburst, embarrassed to

be in his presence alone. "Never mind!" She waved him away and tried to get away from him.

"Wait, Lady Gwynndolen, I should speak with you."

She had to stop and listen; his station required that. But she didn't have to encourage him by looking up into his dark eyes.

"I-I shouldn't have said what I said earlier. I just—"

She waited, but it was painful, and she could feel the night cooling the air around her as the insects hummed. "You . . .?" she prompted at last. She never would have thought the prince, who had been a troubadour before returning to the island of his birth, would be at a loss for words.

He blinked and scrambled for words. "I shouldn't have said it. I hope you will still see fit to help me before we set sail."

She took a deep breath. Was that supposed to be an apology? Fine. "I will do my duty, Your Highness. Now, if you'll excuse me?" Barely moving, Gwynndolen gave the smallest curtsy she could manage before leaving his irksome presence. She flew to her guest chambers and thumped into bed, grateful to be alone. If only she could will herself to sleep before Beatrix returned, but she doubted she would be able to.

⟜⟜⟝⟞⟞

EDMUND SHOOK HIS HEAD. What was wrong with him? Why could he not give a simple apology? He shook his head; he didn't need to stress over trifles tonight. Running into Gwynndolen—literally—was the least of his worries. Why had his mother insisted he meet her down on the shore? It was nearly nightfall, and the castle gates would close soon. Being the prince, he could come and go as he wished, but he didn't like to use his station on such a frivolity. After spending so much of his life serving lords and kings with his gift of song, it now felt unnatural that he had such privileges.

It took little time to find his mother. She had secured a carriage for them, but she wouldn't speak to him, even though they were alone together.

"Mother, what's—"

"Not yet, my son. You must wait till we reach the shore." She had the carriage driver stop well away from the shore, and she insisted they walk together. A weight was lodged against his chest; something felt wrong. It had been a strange day full of misunderstandings. Why must women be difficult? First Gwynndolen struck him when he spoke ill of Rapunzel, then her sister Beatrix plagued him, and now his mother wouldn't explain. Nothing was right. Nothing had been right since Rapunzel spurned him after last year's harvest.

But no—he didn't want to think of that now.

As they approached the shore, he noticed the tide was low, as though someone had pulled the sea back into itself. The waves still lapped the shore, but unhurried. They had left behind a tiny cliff, an indentation in the sand built up by the high tide's pounding and pushing. He knew how the sand must feel, always moved about on the whim of another's desire. The moon shone full up above, casting a glow on the white foam as it rushed up to hug the wet sand. His mother kept walking forward past the tiny cliff, even though he knew her gown would get wet. "Mother, haven't we gone far enough?"

"Almost." The voice was not his mother's, but that of a woman materializing from the waves themselves. In the dim light of the moon, it looked as though it clad her white form in stardust. She shimmered as she came closer, her pale eyes staring at him without blinking.

"Who are——?" His whisper caught in his throat as he stared up at her tall form. He tried again. "Who are you?"

"Have you ever wondered, dear prince, how you came by your bit of magic?"

What was this? Who was she?

"No?" she pressed. The woman's face was unlined, but she seemed older than time. She finished closing the distance between them, though she remained ankle deep in the froth. How could it be that she was otherwise dry? Her long auburn hair hung down her back, and her eyebrows, unplucked, raised in question. "A troubadour who doesn't want to know his own story? I don't believe it."

This startled him, and he could finally sputter, "I know my story! That's why I'm here now. I discovered how Elias the baker stole me and used me for my gift of wish. I've returned to the family I was parted from, set my mother free from her tower, and reconciled her to my father."

"Oh yes, you know that part. You know that part well. But, how did you come by the gift of the wish, little prince?"

As though struck in the chin for the second time that day, he was stunned into silence. This question was too simple and was something he was likely to ask. But he hadn't. Why?

"It was part of your blessing and curse, sweet prince, the sacrifice you will make for me. Let me tell you a little story.

"There was once a young queen. Oh, she was lovely to behold. She had everything she ever wanted, except happiness. How she longed to be happy! To leave behind the shackles of duty. She visited the lords and ladies of her husband's kingdom, and she performed what was necessary each day, each night. She ate what they gave her and smiled with her lips. But her heart—there was something wrong with her heart, wasn't there, Lefwenna?"

A single tear streaked down his mother's face. "Mother?"

"I'm so sorry, my son!"

"Silly prince, your mother came to the shore one night. She was most unhappy. She had discovered she was with child—with you! She was married to a man she didn't love, lived a life she hated—but she wouldn't have a child she didn't want."

His mother's shoulders were shaking, and she whimpered, "Please, stop! Let me tell him—"

The woman from the sea held up her hand. "You should have done, but you didn't. So now he will hear it from me." She turned her ghostly eyes on him once more. "You know who I am, don't you?"

"You are one of the sisters of sorcery—the one confined to the sea."

A devilish smile overtook her lips as she stepped out of the water. "Confined? Yes, but when your mother came to the waters to end her life—"

"To *what?*"

"To *end her life*," she enunciated, "I gave her a wish."

"How? What wish? What did you do to her?"

Her throaty laugh mocked him. "So many questions, we'll take them one by one. I did nothing *to* the queen. Lefwenna came to me, to my waters. She cried out, and I asked her, politely, what she wanted. The clever queen had sewn huge, heavy rocks in her gown, Edmund. But she said she didn't really want to drown. What she wanted was for your father to find her, to love her, and to be the man she wanted him to be. Too bad she didn't ask for that."

"What did she ask for?"

"For you, actually."

"Me?"

The sorceress's lips parted, revealing sharp white teeth. "Yes, when faced with the reality of her own death, she wanted to turn back, but by now, her many gowns had drunk their fill of my waters. She had come further into my realm than she realized. The tide was pulling her out, and those heavy rocks were now within my power. I asked her what she wanted, and she promised that if I saved your life, I could have it. With that, I sent her back to shore, though she must have thought it was all a dream."

"It was a nightmare!"

Edmund frowned at his mother's outburst. "I don't understand, how would that give me—"

Camilla held up a hand. "The power of the wish? She wished for your life, and I wished for you to grow my power each time you spoke a wish. If that fool of a baker hadn't taken you to Alleria, just out of my reach, I should have been freed a long time ago! But now that you have returned, I have gained back a bit of my own. Not all, but enough to hold your life in my hands."

"What is it you want?"

"I hear you leave at first light, a fortnight from now."

"Yes?"

"You are travelling to the High King's court, where my little sister Amee dwells nearby in the marsh." Her eyes grew fevered as she spoke. "Before the summer is over, you will reunite us. The time has come to fulfill *my* wish."

ANOTHER JOURNEY

At first, Rapunzel worried the weather would be too cool for her baby and His Majesty. The wind off the Illyan Sea was far from balmy, she thought. But the king laughed at her expression, his dimples showing. It was a good sign that the king's cheeks were full again. "Come now, it won't be so bad!"

They all climbed aboard a beautiful ship, the king first, then Rapunzel holding Helena, with Paul right behind. Katterina followed next, joined by Jacob, their warrior monk, and last—everyone's favorite—Amis. As the company made their way to the helm, the sailors released the dark blue sails. They were setting out at midmorning, even though Rapunzel had lived long enough in the Fisher King's realm to know that a true fisherman set sail before dawn if he wanted a good catch. Not that she would be terribly excited about setting sail so early, especially with her broken sleep. She wondered if Helena would ever learn to sleep through the night. Perhaps Paul was right when he said they should just bring her to bed with them and not wake in the middle of the night.

She shivered as the wind gusted the sails to blow them out of the harbor, past the inlet. Helena laughed and clapped her hands as they made their way through the waters. Rapunzel gazed into the vast cerulean sky, so blue she felt lost for a moment. Off to the right, a few wispy strands of cloud strayed, but other than that, it was clear. Time passed without Rapunzel taking much notice. It was so peaceful, and Helena was entranced. Before she realized it, they were far enough into the bay that she had to stare hard at the horizon to see the Northlands, but she could still see a bit of Alleria wrapping around from the East and to the South. The sailors barked orders across the deck and dropped anchor as they lowered the sails. Helena giggled again as several birds soared through the air, cawing. Their black beaks and the black tips of their wings contrasted with their white bodies. The little one reached up as though to fly with them herself.

The Fisher King laughed as sailors threw a net over the side. "Yes, Helena, it is a beautiful day filled with lovely creatures. And now, it's been too long since we gathered you together. We and the other kings of the Northlands are forever in your debt for saving us, our person and our kingdom, from Ute."

Jacob's dark skin shone in the sun, his clean-shaven tonsure a testament to his faith, his expression proving he was a warrior monk, even if he wasn't wearing his chain mail. Highly prized by his king, the firm man chose his words carefully, so the king inclined his head when Jacob cleared his throat. "Yes, brother?"

"You've honored us before your court for our part in freeing you from the curse. Why would you need to gather us together again?"

"Well, we have things to discuss. You've each been so

busy since returning that we've hardly had this group together again. We suppose we could have commanded it, but we felt you all needed time. Prince Paul and Princess Rapunzel had to learn their place in our court and tend to little Helena. And all of you needed time to heal your wounds. Over the winter, though, we have thought things over, and we feel it's important that you are all together for our next decision."

Rapunzel didn't know why, but she held her breath and tightened her hold on Helena.

"We are finally well enough to be away from our sickbed and out among the waters again, but the curse took its toll. We'll never be the same as we once were. It's time to give the kingdom over to you, Paul."

Paul moved forward as though to say something, but the king, refusing the interruption, held up his hand to hold off his nephew. "Let us finish before you try to change our mind. There are many things we've thought through about running this kingdom, many things you need to know. Would we want you to learn all those lessons as soon as we've died, or while we are still alive and able to guide you?

"And here is why the rest of you have all been called together. You make an excellent team, and Paul will need that support. Brother Jacob, Paul will need spiritual guidance and further training. A king must always be ready to defend his kingdom. And"—he shrugged his shoulder a bit—"there may be things you disagree with us about. We don't want that to get in the way. You make the best decisions you can. You have our support, and Jacob's.

"There are also things we've never had time to do because we were so young when we became king. Perhaps, as our health improves, we can enjoy life better once we have handed the burden over to you. We'll need help with that,

Amis. Of all our servants, you know the most about enjoying life."

"That I do, Your Majesty!" The cheeky jester laughed, his dark blue fool's cap bobbing.

"No running back to Maer to serve Lord Col unless we give you leave. We have things for you to do!" The king joined his laughter—then cleared his throat self-consciously as he looked over at the two women.

"Princess Rapunzel, we cannot pretend to understand what it is you will need to learn to become queen. Lady Katterina, we know you didn't raise her with this goal in mind. How could you have? There has, however, come an invitation—actually a command—for us all. Since the High Queen has finally given the High King a son, they are to hold court a year early for the christening. We are sending you with Paul to represent the kingdom and to receive the High King's blessing as the new king and queen. Once there, you will choose a suitable lady-in-waiting, trained at court. She will return home with you and serve you.

"We, Paul and ourself, have spoken of this thing, and we know it is difficult, but you must see to it. He also says that you may know where in Alleria Helena's family is from."

Rapunzel couldn't answer, at first, as her throat tightened. She could finally swallow. "I knew her family when they met together at their deceased mother's home to unravel the witch's curse."

"Then, while you are traveling, you will go there and return Helena to her rightful family. This will resolve the kingdom's debt."

"But she is so young to be—"

The king held up his hand. Rapunzel's eyes stung as she darted a glance at Paul. How long had he known this new journey would be undertaken?

"Your mother and your servant should accompany you to help care for the child, since you must bring her with you."

This was something she could object to. "But I won't be needing Jehanne! She is an obedient servant, but Helena only responds to me."

Paul's wide hazel eyes warned Rapunzel she had spoken out of turn, but the king took no offense and merely chuckled. "We wondered if you might object. We do not pretend it will be a simple journey, but, Paul, we have already spoken with Jacob about all that your company will need to make it overland. You can leave in two days' time."

"In two days!" Rapunzel squeezed Helena, causing the wee one to squirm.

"Yes, and as we've said, Brother Jacob has readied things. Your servants will pack you ladies up, and you can set off. Don't look so dismayed, dear Rapunzel—the journey ahead is not fraught with danger. You will have Paul and the escort of Jacob's knights to guard you and our tribute. Your mother will help with Helena and—"

"I must go as well!" Amis sprang into action, flipping his way across the ship's deck and then back, landing before the king with his animated eyebrows wriggling. Rapunzel marveled that he had stayed quiet for such a long time. And how did he make his body move like that and manage not to smash into a single sailor?

"Oh, no, our little fool. We need you here."

"I'm sorry, my king—I make up part of this team, and they will need me for what is ahead."

"What could be ahead? Ute isn't waiting at the end of this road, just a drunk High King and his high-strung wife."

Amis laughed and clapped his hands. "Ute is dead, it is true, but they will still need me."

Only Amis could refuse the king's order and make the man laugh at the same time. Rapunzel forced a smile to her face and breathed in the salt air while Helena reached for Paul. Her mind conjured images of traveling southeast from the Northlands, through Alleria, to reach the Eastern Ports— but such a journey seemed too great. She wanted to take comfort in the thought that Ute and her witch were dead, but her heart ached at the thought of losing Helena partway through the upcoming trip.

LEARNING

$\mathcal{E}$dmund approached Gwynndolen from the castle through the dew-wet field. The morning air was chill, and he took in a breath of it as he tried to measure the maid's features. From what he could see, she wore her face like battle armor, as though she were a knight riding in to defeat a foe. Perhaps she should be the one to fight in the High King's tournament. But she had been adopted and made a lady and would instead have to watch the contestants. Ironic that though she was a lady, her prowess in maneuvering a horse was so good that it was known throughout Rona that she could teach any man to ride and still handle a weapon at the same time. Even her brothers referred those whose skills were lacking to their younger sister. And Edmund's skills were sorely lacking.

"Good morning, Your Highness."

"Lady Gwynndolen," Edmund replied stiffly at her sharp tone.

She dropped her gaze and swallowed. "My brothers said that before we cross the sea, you would like to receive some instruction on how to better—" But she hesitated.

"How to better what?"

She shook her head and grimaced. Being civil must not come naturally to this one. "To maneuver your steed. They said you were having difficulty, especially when fighting."

Did he have to answer? Of course—why not admit to all of his flaws? "Yes, well, there was little cause for me to learn and practice such things when I sang for my bread. I mostly traveled from hearth to hearth, and only with a steed when the money was plentiful."

Her hard gaze softened a tad, and she gave a single nod, gesturing for him to follow. She led him to a strong caramel-colored mare who snuffed Gwynndolen affectionately. Gwynndolen handed him the reins. "This is my mare. She is gentle and responds favorably to commands. Trust yourself with her, and you won't have trouble." Saying this, she mounted her stallion astride, her lavender full skirt providing no resistance while her legs were protected by matching hosen, much like the ones he wore daily. She arched an unplucked eyebrow when she caught him looking at her. "You look surprised, Your Highness."

"I don't know what to make of a lady who rides like a man."

Her grin slipped slightly. He had done it again, hadn't he? "Perhaps riding a horse is no more a male thing than eating is. It's all in how you do it. Now, I believe it is you who came to me for help."

Edmund mounted after transferring his sword to the saddle sheath, and they headed further afield where they could work. He pushed through the motions of guiding the mare this way and that, unsheathing his sword and advancing. But he felt like rusted armor, his movements mechanical when compared the fluidity of Gwynndolen as she surprised him over and again when they clashed swords.

Finally, she sheathed her short sword and rode up to meet him. "Have you ever hunted, Your Highness?"

He fumbled with re-sheathing his sword. "Yes, but only once while mounted."

Her face pinched slightly. "Were you successful?"

He didn't want to lie. "Quite, but it was not because of my ability to ride."

"What do you mean?"

"You don't—it's not pertinent that you know. Can't you teach me without more questions?"

"Well, that makes it harder. If I don't know your experience with a horse, I'm uncertain what I need to do to help you."

"Please, just teach me what I need to know so I won't make a fool of myself at court this summer."

She huffed a sigh and blew a curl of hair out of her face. "Oh! Is that all you're worried about?"

For one moment, a slanted grin took over his face. "If there were a tournament for a prince who could sing for the court, I could bring honor to my father, but as it stands, I have nothing to give him."

Gwynndolen's steed stomped, and she frowned. "Your father had no heir he knew of, but now he has you. Haven't you seen how he presents you with pride?"

"I squandered that honor when I hurt and lost Rapunzel. I'll never be the man I should be."

"No one could be who speaks like that! I'm sorry, Your Highness, but you've only yourself to blame for your mistakes. Any of us can be different, can choose to be better!"

He couldn't believe her ire.

"With God's help," she added, a little late.

"Of course," he said, looking away.

"Fine. We'll just get on with the lesson, shall we?"

"That would be preferable."

THE CLOUDS momentarily uncovered the midday sun, and it glinted its light on a single strand of cobweb, the gossamer thread waving in the wind. Amee's equine eyes followed the glint without blinking and watched the web quiver as a fly got caught in its net. The spider, too, was watching from up in a corner of the web. As the fly struggled and strained, the spider crept out, its long legs tickling down the side of the web, and wrapped the fly up tight.

Amee looked away, sniffing the air, her opaque eyes darting as she listened. A breeze caught at the tufts of hanging moss suspended from the sprawling branches. The air hummed with insect life. Even in the dead of winter, the marsh had been alive with insects, but now as spring blew her warm breath and stirred the thick waters, the insects were a buzzing orchestra.

Mauro approached, across the waters. She could hear the oar dipping in and out of the marsh. His dark curly beard covered his mahogany face—but when had it become patched with grey? Had it been that way last week when they had met? The clouds again covered the sun. His eyes widened when she moved enough for him to differentiate her from the shadows beneath the sprawling tree.

"My Lady," he said with a low bow, deftly balancing in the boat, as all her people of these parts could.

She acquiesced her acknowledgment with a nod of her head. One might never suspect how she had trusted this man with her last precious gift long ago. Even she didn't know for sure where that gift was. Only when the ache became too deep did she spy him out to satisfy her longing with a quick glance. But no more. It was the only way to make certain it had remained hidden from her sisters. "What have you learned?"

"As you suspected, the gathering will be this summer and not next. The queen has had a son at last, and now the kings and queens are coming to celebrate. But something has gone amiss in the Northlands—"

"I knew it!"

"My Lady?"

"I'm sorry—proceed." She lifted her head back to its regal position. She mustn't interrupt her messenger, but she wanted to squeal with glee. Ute did it! She did it! The weight of an entire season of fear lifted off Amee, and she listened intently as he entailed how their people were doing.

"Then, the sacrifice we made long ago was worth it." She kept her tone even. Emotions were intolerable, especially if they would require another sacrifice to reignite the war.

The dark man nodded his head, but not before a tear swam its way down his cheek and disappeared into his curly beard. "I'm afraid that our sacrifice was not the only one."

"What do you mean?"

BATTLES AHEAD

By midday, they returned to the castle, having both worked up a sweat guiding their horses through different motions. Edmund had begun to feel how to engage his hips and use his thighs and the reins to tell the horse where he wanted to go. Gwynndolen had done nothing too daring, but she could see that, though he might deny it, he had a good way with her mare. His stiff movements had softened and revealed his comfort with horses, even if he hadn't been properly trained. She was fairly certain that his problem lay in the idea of the battle itself, which had little to do with the horse.

She wished she could fight for him. How she would enjoy the rush! Because of her father's long illness, she had worked alongside her brothers, and though they gave her a hard time, they insisted she was the best at training the horses properly. They were good themselves, having learned, like Gwynndolen, from their father before he became ill. She was glad they let her learn many unladylike things—and that her mother allowed it all. The poor woman had enough to worry over with her husband's illness, and she seemed proud of her daughter's skills.

"Oh, Gwynn! You smell like the stables!" Beatrix pinched her nose with her fingers when Gwynndolen passed her in a castle corridor. "You'd best clean up and have the servants bring you mid-meal. If Mother were here instead of home with father, she would be horrified for the king to smell you reeking with such a stench. It's not even summer yet!"

"No, but it was good and hot once the sun came out this morning. Besides, the king should be happy. I spent the entire time training his son. He won't be perfect before we leave for the Eastern Ports, but he should be able to hold his own in the tournament with the other princes."

Beatrix leaned in, her pupils darkening. "Oh, I hope so. I would dearly hate our prince to be a laughingstock."

"So it's good that I smell, dear sister, isn't it?" She didn't wait for a reply, but headed to their chambers, asking a maidservant on the way to attend her. She was grateful not to dine with the others. Once in the evening was enough to fill her with more boredom than she longed for. She would rather be outside!

As she finished cleaning up, she heard a knock on her chamber's door. Back in the garb that most women wore, she deemed herself presentable and allowed her maidservant to grant the visitor entrance. There in the doorway stood the petite queen. But she looked troubled.

Gwynndolen bowed before addressing her aunt. "Your Majesty? Are you all right?"

The woman came in and murmured for the maidservant to leave. The door made a gentle thud as it closed, but the queen stood motionless in the center of the room.

"Your Majesty?" Gwynndolen prompted again after several minutes had passed.

"Gwynndolen . . ."

"Yes?"

Finally, the queen's Ronan eyes focused on hers. "I have a favor to ask of you."

"Yes?"

"Would you—I need you to endear yourself to my son."

Gwynndolen felt her mouth drop open. "I'm sorry —what?"

All at once, the queen could move again. She walked over to the bed that the girls shared, and she untied the curtains from the bedposts as though interested in the garish orange silk. "I see how your sister has set her eyes on my son, but that would not be a suitable match. My son is too vulnerable right now. He needs a woman of substance, someone who will not allow him to overwhelm her. What the prince needs is a woman who knows her own mind and won't allow him to change it."

"Wh-why me?"

The queen dropped the curtain and walked over to her niece. She placed her hands on the young maid's shoulders.

"It's not as though you are of the same blood, but you are noble, and my sister did well when she chose to bring you into the family. All this time with your father ill, you have been helping. You've been training horses and battling your brothers to keep things in order. They are good boys—young men, really—but except for Georgius, they haven't taken the responsibility as well as you. You have managed things and maintained order."

"How do you know this?"

"When I was imprisoned, I prayed a great deal for you. God let me see some of what your family went through and how you rose to meet those challenges." Her hand lifted, tucking a loose strand of red hair behind Gwynndolen's ear. "You are the maid my son needs at his side."

"I am—uh—flattered that Your Majesty would consider me a worthy—uh—"

"Wife."

"Um—yes, and—uh—future . . ." but now it was her turn to get stuck and stare dumbly.

Her aunt lifted Gwynndolen's chin with a gentle finger as she said in a hushed voice, "It would make you the future queen of Rona."

"But I don't even know that I *wish* to marry. I don't want to go to court! I'm only going to the Eastern Ports for the horses. And because my mother insists. I'd much rather stay at home—care for the horses. Keep things managed."

"Which is why I want you for his wife."

"But I don't understand."

The queen laughed, and the sound of her laughter warmed Gwynndolen despite their serious subject. "No, but that's because you don't understand *him* yet. And you don't understand yourself, yet, either. You will soon see how you fit together."

"What does the prince say? I can't imagine he would want—"

"Oh, silly girl, the prince doesn't know, nor the king. But the king will agree, eventually. I know the prince's heart and what he needs for the days ahead. He will need you to help him battle."

"Battle what?"

"I cannot say, but it will require a maid who is brave— and that, my dear, is you."

SWORDPLAY

*J*acob was glad for Paul's insistence that they go to the courtyard to train one last time. There would be plenty of riding for weeks on end, but some training before they left would do them both good. Besides, Jacob could see that Paul had something he needed to speak about. Like most men, the young prince would well discuss it with a weapon in hand.

The two men measured one another while circling around. Paul was dropping his right shoulder. When he stepped back with the same foot, Jacob had already expected his rush and so feinted with ease. Turning to face Paul, the warrior monk was pleased to see the young man was taking it in stride. His counter was quick, sword raised and ready for Jacob to come at him. But Jacob shook his head with a smile and kept on defense. Paul laughed and rushed him again, though this time it was more like a game when Jacob stepped out of the way. Now both men were laughing. Paul needed this release. He had had too little sleep between the wakeful baby and the additional responsibilities being thrust on his shoulders.

The men then settled on a rhythm of thrust and parry, strike and defend. They were panting hard by the time Paul finally had the upper hand and Jacob yielded. The older man smiled at the younger. "Well done! I suppose you will represent the kingdom in the tournament this time."

"I hadn't thought they would have one."

"Really? A chance for the High King to measure all the princes and kings beneath him while he drinks and drinks?"

Paul laughed as he wiped sweat from his forehead. "I suppose I should see things that way, shouldn't I?"

"Now that you are to be king, you should." The prince nodded in silence, and Jacob's wide lips stretched into a rare smile. He clapped his hand on the young man's back. That was what he liked about Paul. The prince was wise in evaluating things he wasn't certain of. He also knew to take counsel only from those who had proven trustworthy.

"One day, Your Highness, you will have an heir to represent you."

Paul didn't answer right away as they stood facing each other. "What if I had a daughter for an heir?"

"Not unheard of—but she must be yours."

Paul nodded, his eyes downcast.

Jacob started walking to the castle's armory, and Paul followed. "How is Princess Rapunzel?"

"Angry, upset. She knew we would return Helena when her family came this summer—but going to find them ourselves—? And the fact that I have discussed this with the king and not her . . ." His voice trailed off.

"She will have to grow used to some of these things. You can't discuss all the affairs of court with her when your sovereign does not allow it. And even when you are king, you still may need to keep some things to yourself."

Paul shrugged and shook his head. "I'm so new to being a husband, and this business with losing Helena—"

Jacob wondered if the prince had forgotten how to complete his sentences. He decided it was best to change subjects. "You know, should you have only daughters, your heir may lack the support of the High King. Think how long he has waited for his own son."

Paul tried to smile, grateful to speak of anything else. "That is accurate enough. I will tell Rapunzel we can only have sons. Especially if we want one to represent us before the High King in the tournament!" Paul attempted a half-hearted laugh.

"Don't laugh too hard—I have known women warriors who swept my feet out from under me. I hope you won't be humbled in such a way."

"What warriors?"

"They come from the south, the land of my ancestors."

Paul nodded to the guard that opened the armory door for them. "The Land of Midnight?" He spoke in a reverent tone. No one underestimated the power of the warriors, but neither had any dared go to the continent since the plague struck. Jacob, like the rest of those alive, had never even seen the shape of the land. All trade with the continent south of the High King's lands had ceased two centuries before, and the handsome, dark-skinned traders and warriors trapped in the Eastern Ports at the time had made new homes there.

Jacob's race of people resigned themselves to making a different life far from the land they had loved. Many had intermarried with their fair-skinned neighbors, culminating in what was now the culture of the Eastern Ports. Jacob's ancestors had been the original missionaries to share the Good News of Jesu, the Christ. They had instituted the original monastery in the Eastern Ports where the Father now lived and maintained the order of warrior monks. From there the missionaries had set up churches throughout Alleria and the Northlands, converting as they went. But that had been centuries before the plague, even more centuries before the War of Sorcery, when the church finally took arms against the darkness opposed to the light of God. There had been rumors during the War of Sorcery that some witches and wizards had escaped to the southern continent, but no one knew for certain. None dared to find out if any civilization had survived the plague.

"It will be good to return to the Eastern Ports, you know," Jacob continued, his dark brows lowered in memory. "I haven't returned since I was a very young man."

"How long did it take, coming here?" Paul asked, cleaning his sword with a soft cloth.

"The route we took up into the Soontrisse Mountains took us a month or more. I imagine with a small child and the women, this journey will take at least as long."

Paul nodded again, but his hazel eyes clouded with thought. "I am glad to take everyone, but part of me—"

Jacob did not let the young husband finish his sentence, but put his sword away with a sigh. "I know, it complicates things to take women and a babe along. We will be glad for the company, but it will slow us down."

Paul's smile was sheepish. "I wouldn't want Rapunzel or Katterina to hear me say that."

"No. They are both good travelers, but it is different and much faster when it is just men."

"And safer."

"Yes, and safer."

The men remained silent for another moment as they finished, but Jacob felt the need to speak before they returned their weapons. "Paul, the Fisher King is sending me to do more than just keep you safe on the journey. All of us will report to the High King about our little adventure this last fall. But it's not just the High King who needs to know. The Father of the Church must hear from me about Ute.

She was one of three, and she did such damage without a connection to her sisters. There's no telling what the other two are trying to do even after her death."

"Why didn't—"

"I asked your uncle to let me tell you privately. There will be tough decisions for us to make, but no need to alarm the women." A frown flickered across Paul's features. "If you feel you need to say something—"

Paul shook his head slowly and said, "There's really nothing to say at this point."

A BETTER MAN

$\mathcal{P}$rince Edmund was scowling for most of his lesson, concentration a mask of worry across his features. Gwynndolen's mare was listening to his commands and allowing him to guide her, but Gwynndolen knew that if he would lighten his grip and allow himself to enjoy the ride, things would go better.

She rode up next to him. "Let's just walk for a moment." Instantly, the prince's clenched jaw relaxed. "Um, how did you become a troubadour?" Gwynndolen wasn't sure why she was making conversation, but there was tension in the air. She had a tendency to fill tense moments with inane remarks. The prince's mouth quirked into his sideways smile.

"I'm sure the kingdom knows this story after my travels around the island last summer. Wasn't there a great deal of gossip?"

"To tell the truth, Your Highness, I wasn't much interested in you or your story."

"I don't find that difficult to believe at all."

"No?"

"You don't seem to care much about what other ladies at court worry over."

Gwynndolen wasn't sure if this was good or bad. "Well, that's true. I find sitting around and gossiping a dull pastime when I could be outside with the horses in the fresh air accomplishing something."

The prince nodded.

"So . . .?"

"I'm sure you at least heard about the baker who stole me from my parents?"

"Yes, that was why the king imprisoned the queen, because the baker made it look as though wild animals killed you while she napped nearby."

"Right, so I grew up doing the baker's bidding. I have certain talents he found . . . useful."

"What talents could a mere—"

A strange look crossed the prince's face, and he pulled up his horse in the middle of the field where they'd been walking the horses. "Gwynndolen, I can make things happen. All I have to do is wish for them."

Gwynndolen frowned and spoke the only word that made sense: "What?"

"I—I have this ability to make a wish and it has to come true. People have to do what I want."

"Being a prince and future king isn't enough? You have to have some strange ability to command obedience?"

"I didn't ask for it! It was forced on me."

"*Forced* on you?"

"I had no choice. I was born this way."

"Do you have the choice to abstain from—wait, were you controlling Rapunzel?"

He didn't reply, but nudged his horse to walk again.

Gwynndolen rode up beside him. "You were, weren't

you? And then she left, so she got away from your power. She left you and you couldn't stop her!"

"I didn't want to try . . . anymore."

"'Anymore'?"

"You're right, I was controlling her. What I did to Rapunzel was wrong—but I didn't set out to do it."

"Well then, that makes it just *fine*."

"I haven't used my wish often—and I've only used it once since Rapunzel left!"

Gwynndolen could tell her expression wasn't helping matters, but she didn't care. "Why tell me?"

"I don't know, you were a friend to Rapunzel and I don't want to be the man—the *king* that would ever do something like that again."

A space of quiet fell between them, only interrupted by the soft thumping of the horse's hooves on the fresh spring grass.

Finally, Gwynndolen spoke. "I still don't understand why you would tell me."

"I just wanted someone to know. And, you've made it clear what you think of me. I wanted you to know I'm trying to be a better man." He let that sink in, and Gwynndolen looked at him. "When I was a troubadour, I could just sing my songs and go from place to place and disappoint no one. My life was my own. But now that I've entangled myself with others who depend upon me, I've made a mess of things."

Gwynndolen shifted in her saddle. "My brothers don't think so. They'd be happy to follow you into battle if need be. And my sister—well, Beatrix looks on you with favor."

"Is that what it is?"

Gwynndolen couldn't help the unexpected laugh that burst forth, but she stopped immediately, pretending to cough.

"Well, I could do without her favor. It's not the kind I'm

looking for. I don't want everyone to know what I can do or why I was stolen, but I just want—" He shrugged.

"To be better?"

"Yes."

"Then you will." Gwynndolen looked away with a frown. Is that what she wanted for him? Her lower lip disappeared into her mouth as she bit it. She knew she wanted Edmund to be an upstanding man for her aunt, someone who would fight this battle and win. "Besides," she couldn't seem to keep from adding, "I doubt you could control everyone. Some of us are stronger than others."

"Are you daring me to try?"

"I'm promising you'll regret it if you try."

He held up a gloved hand in defense. "I have no desire to control you, Gwynndolen. I've learned the cost."

She nodded and turned her horse around as she said, "Let's head back. I'd say we've both learned enough this morning."

LOSS AND SACRIFICE

Amee blinked, but she could not keep the sob from erupting. Gone. How could Ute be gone? When the portal had closed, she had never dreamed it meant Ute had died.

Ute. Dead. Ute, the strong, the capable, the cunning.

Her eldest sister's prodding had kept Amee from despair when their mother had died at their father's hands. She had lost hope when they fell under the curse, separated, over fifty years ago. But even so, Ute had formed a plan and found a way. Amee remembered the first time the witch Eufemia, Ute's pupil, had found her and brought word of the plan. Amee had understood her part—to raise a group of followers immersed in the ways of dark magic. As they grew in strength and number, she sent them out to infiltrate the common people and prepare for the war ahead. Even when Eufemia disappeared, Ute's magic had finally grown to such strength that it connected them for a few hours. Then the connection broke. There would be no war now, would there?

A gaping hole of emotion swallowed Amee as she felt the

tears rise to the surface. She closed her eyes and allowed her spirit to concentrate, finding the energy she would need. She found it deep inside the roots of trees and allowed her physical form to morph. First, her body stretched tall before doubling over, her neck sprouting a new set of shoulders with brand new arms. Her feet and hands became hooves that stomped the earth, impatient for the transformation to complete. Old arms and legs grew fine horsehair that covered Amee's whole body up to her neck and new torso. Eager to be off, she began galloping hard between the trees, trunks flying past as her hooves skipped over roots. She was careful to avoid the soft spots of the marsh, trying to escape the pain tearing at her chest.

How could her sister die? Who had done this thing? Who had killed her?

Camilla thought Amee too quiet, too weak, but Ute had said quiet could be strong. But Ute was gone. Now there was nothing; she had followers for a plan that no longer existed. Had she sacrificed her beloved firstborn for nothing? Without Ute, she could not connect with Camilla and they could not follow the plan. They were lost.

She didn't see her maidservant until it was almost too late. Amee reared up on her hind legs to keep from trampling her.

"My lady!" the young woman cried in fear.

Amee swiped angrily at her tear-streaked face and shrank down to stand on two legs. She wrapped herself in a gown of green so dark it blended in with the shades of twilight now descending on them.

"My Lady," Nofra repeated reverently as she bowed low. Her dark braid cascaded over a shoulder and nearly touched the ground.

Amee tried to calm her voice as she answered, "I thought you were back with the rest of the coven, preparing—"

"I was, but when Mauro told me what happened last winter, I worried for you."

Amee didn't know where to look. This lovely mortal was precious to her. Amee had kept her close all her life, doted on her, knowing the destiny Nofra might have—and regretting it. The young woman had heart and soul, a kindness that could undo Amee right now. If the pain of Ute's loss hit her, she might lose her mind. She must focus, must think. Amee had never wanted to lead, but now she needed to. There was nothing else to do.

"You should not have come!" she lashed out, and Nofra stepped back. "It is too important that you do exactly as you've been told."

The maid no longer dared look her in the eye, which helped Amee. She knew she could now observe her, reassess what use she could be now. The maid was tall and willowy, dark as night despite her mixed heritage, with curly hair pulled into the side braid symbolic of all who served Amee's covens. "Yes, my mother, you are right. I don't know what I was thinking. I should never have—"

Amee held up a hand as she imagined Ute would have done. "Stop. I don't need your regrets, only your promise that you will return and do your duty. Think of your people and how you should serve them now—serve me now." Her voice broke, but she blinked her weakness away. "We will find a way. Your life will still serve us. Return to your home and wait for my decision."

The maid kept her eyes lowered a moment more and then looked up through the dim light. Night came faster in the marsh beneath the canopy of fresh leaves. "I will return, but are you going to be—"

"I'll be fine, as long as we see this through."

"Yes."

For a moment, Amee was tempted to accept the comfort

being offered by the kind arms that had momentarily reached for her. She wanted to bend, to be a person again, to let go of the anger, the hatred, even the power that held her to this path. But they had sacrificed too much. She had lost too much. She could barely breathe as she thought of her last image of Ute as the sorceress drew the power from the trio above the swirling waters. What had gone wrong? How could she make it right? Amee wouldn't be able to rest until she knew.

PROWLING THE GARDENS

After the evening meal, Katterina wandered outside to the castle's garden. It was already growing dark, but a few lanterns were lit nearby, showing the tulips that were peeping up in their raised beds near the scrubby bushes, almost ready to open. The gardeners would soon work, but Katterina liked that they had let things rest during the winter. She felt more at peace here despite the chill than in the tidy and warm greenhouse that Rapunzel loved.

She noticed Jacob come striding up while she was stretching her legs. Katterina smiled to herself. In the days ahead, she would feel imprisoned in a carriage with minimal time for walking, since she would be helping Rapunzel with Helena. But time with the child would be short, so she tried to count it all joy, as the monk had taught her to do.

She looked up and smiled at the man. Often they would just stand together in silence. It was unique to have someone like him in her life with whom words were unnecessary. But tonight, she tilted her head to the side as she said, "It has occurred to me we are returning to your home. Have you missed it?"

"Occasionally. But I haven't thought of it as my home for a very long time."

"No?"

"No. Once I hardened myself to endure the cold winters of the Northlands, I made my home here. Surprisingly, I even enjoy winter now. I have looked on the Fisher King as my lord and king and his people as those I am to guide and protect ever since I was a young man."

"I suppose you will visit the monastery while we are in the Eastern Ports, won't you?" Jacob stared at Katterina. She stared back, her luminescent green eyes unblinking, and smiled again. "What?" she asked, as warmth filled her cheeks. How could she feel so young, though she was old enough that her daughter was married?

"I would like you to come with me to see the Father."

"The Father! Do you know him personally?"

"I have known him a long time, long before he became the Father. He was the one who decided I should come to the Northlands to smash the wicked altar in the Soontrisse Mountains."

"What is he like?"

"He is tall, or seemed to be when I was young. His skin isn't as dark as mine, it's olive-toned. I imagine after all this time, his hair will be gr—"

Katterina laughed, and Jacob stopped. "That's not what I meant. I heard stories of him and his predecessors when I was a little girl going to Mass. What was he like, as a priest?"

"Well, he was stern, strong, and considered nothing beneath him. Once a year, he insisted on travelling to out-of-the-way convents to hear the confessions of the nuns and help them celebrate the Christ Mass. I always liked that about him. He was straightforward and didn't abide fools, cowards, or heretics."

She hesitated a moment before asking what filled her

with dread. The past held so much power. "What about sisters of witches?"

"You need not worry—he is in your debt. You and I defeated Ute together."

Katterina gave another nod and stared at him with her cat-like intensity. "Why did you never return?"

"I was told that many of us needed to stay in the North-lands, and returning to the Eastern Ports . . . Well, I had just discovered the shame my mother brought on our family with her witchcraft. I thought I needed to bear the weight of her guilt. I know now that there was no grace from God in my thinking, but I suppose I was paying penance of some sort. I denied myself everything—excellent wine, fine food, love—"

"Love?"

"I made my vow of chastity in the wake of this new knowledge. I felt if I denied myself love and a family, I would somehow make up for my mother's treachery."

Katterina's eyes filled with tears, and her voice was husky when she said, "I have tried to pay penance, too. It doesn't work that way, though, does it?"

"Jesu the Christ paid the price for our sins once and for all with his death and resurrection. We need only accept. When we don't, we only hurt the ones who try to love us." He closed his eyes tight. What was he remembering? What love had he denied himself? He cleared his throat. "I should finish making us ready for the morning. I—I'm glad we spoke."

"I'm always glad to speak with you, Jacob." A tear clung to her lashes, but he turned away as though he hadn't seen it, giving her time to recollect herself.

REGRET AND FORGIVENESS

*E*dmund didn't want to see her, but the queen came to him anyway. Her soft knock was easy to answer, and there she stood in the doorway of his bedchamber, looking ashamed. Unusual. Her head was uncovered, and her long auburn hair was plaited with pink ribbons complementing the few streaks of silver. She came into the room and looked around, her high forehead giving no indication that she had ever seen the room before. It was a normal bedchamber reserved for honored guests. A large bed dominated the center of the room with turquoise and orange silk curtains hanging from the canopy. A single west-facing window cast a sidelong latticed ray of light across a thick orange rug on the floor. Edmund found it hideous.

"Son?" The queen turned to him, and he looked into her tear-filled eyes. He tried to imagine the hurting young woman she had been. How miserable would someone have to be to want to end their own life? He didn't mean to step back, but he did. She stopped advancing toward him and dropped the trembling hand that had been reaching out to touch him. "I—I wanted to say I'm sorry."

"You need not say anything."

"I do! If I had not been so foolish as to try to drown—"

"Mother!" He turned away as though the action could shut his ears to her words of regret. That she had ever— "Had you hated a child so much?"

"I hated living, not you!" Her voice poured out in a warm rush. "I didn't think of you as a person until the moment I was certain I would lose my life. I couldn't fathom being queen to a man who despised me. How could I imagine birthing and raising his child?" She took a deep breath as a stream of tears wet her face. "You don't understand—let me try to explain. My mother was a beautiful woman, but hard-hearted. She played at court, as did my father. They made each other miserable, and my sister and me as well. I didn't know how Genevieve became the sweet woman she is . . . I thought I would make you—I thought it would be kinder if I could just make it all stop." Her eyes drifted away from his face as her hands clasped each other in a tight knot. Did those same hands remember choosing the rocks and sewing them into her cotehardie before wading out into the waters?

"Did you know I could wish for things?"

She nodded. "You learned to speak at an early age. That's how our baker found out. You had a sweet tooth as a child."

"Yes, well, he cured me of that."

"What do you mean?"

"It was how he would entice me to make wishes for him —he would make something good for me to eat. But I realized it came with a price." He didn't want to remember, though. His time with the baker was dark and horrible. He needed to be free of this conversation. "Mother, what is it you need from me?"

"Your forgiveness." She let the words hang in the air, and

Edmund stared at her. Did he hate her for what she had done? How could he? "I never knew the woman who tried to —you are someone new and different now." But still, he had suffered from her mistake.

"I am someone different, but only because God changed me. He does that for us when we trust him."

Edmund waved away the thought of the God who had allowed her to suffer. He walked to the window and looked out, seeing the grounds below where Gwynndolen was exercising a horse. "Mother, I *do* forgive you. There is only one snag. It will be hard to forgive my father for allowing you to be so unhappy."

"But I've told you I was as much to blame as he was."

He turned back with a scowl in his voice. "I think a man should be able to make his wife happy."

She gave a half-hearted laugh and placed a hand on his shoulder. "If only it were that easy. I think it takes two to make a good marriage, son, and we have only recently been learning how to do that."

Edmund nodded and thought of Rapunzel and the marriage he had wanted to have with her. Strange—he now thought of her as someone from another life. She had never really been his. The marriage would not have been happy because he could never have made her love him. It still hurt, but it was a dull ache, leaving a longing for something else, something true.

"I hear"—the queen cleared her throat and looked down at Gwynndolen—"your lessons in weaponry and riding have been going well."

Edmund was grateful to speak of something else. "Yes, the king was wise to ask that I receive further training from my cousins. They have been a great help."

"I thought you were already a good rider."

"Not battle-worthy, mother."

"So you learn battle riding from a maid?"

Did his mother have to look at him like that? "Have you ridden with your niece?"

"I haven't."

"She is as fiery as her hair, perhaps more so."

Now she was laughing. "And I've heard she can hit, too."

"Yes, well . . ." He touched his jaw gently. "I deserved it."

"And you made amends?"

"As much as I can."

"Well, it's nice that you have made friends. We'll all be seeing a great deal of each other through the summer. I'm asking them to stay during the tournament after they deliver the horses to the High King."

Edmund turned from the window to look at the queen. "Stay? What for?"

"Your cousins need to make suitable matches and, given our connections at the High Court, staying will be to their advantage. After all their family has been through, I hope, at least, to see to it the girls make good marriages."

"They are fair enough."

"Especially Beatrix?" His mother tilted her head as if there was more to the question.

Edmund shrugged. "She will make someone happy, I'm sure."

"And Gwynndolen?"

He snorted. "I hope her future husband knows how to duck."

"Or hold his tongue."

"Yes, well, most men don't. He'd best have good reflexes."

"Perhaps that will just make life more interesting for them."

Why was she looking at him like that? "Perhaps."

"Just promise you'll look out for her."

"You should have me promise to look out for the men left behind in her wake." He expected her to laugh, but she didn't. "You're serious? And should I look out for Beatrix as well?"

"No—I think if you look out for Gwynndolen then all will go well with us."

⁂

THE MORNING SKY was dark and grey when they started out. Helena, normally a happy baby in the morning, was fussy. Rapunzel had had to give her over to Jehanne to coddle so she could finish getting ready in time, but she hated even that small bit of defeat. Shouldn't she always be able to care for Helena herself? She snatched back her child—the child —as quick as her hands were free. Had Katterina lived a normal life with Rapunzel's father, she never would have hired anyone to help care for Rapunzel. Why should Rapunzel need help now? Not that Helena belonged to Rapunzel and Paul, but this was the last time they had left with her.

The first leg of the journey took only a day to cross the Bay of Trisse on the king's ship. The brief trip cut days off the overland route. Though she was grateful to shorten their travel time, the trip by water made her nervous. There had been rumors of strangers taking to the sea and capturing vessels. She had thought these stories mere tall tales, but now she wondered.

Paul laughed at her when she breathed a sigh of relief as they set foot on Allerian soil the next morning. "Rapunzel, were you concerned about pirates?"

She gave a small nod. "I didn't want to say anything."

"I wondered why you were eating so little. You could have told me, and I would have relieved your fears. They don't tour the bay, they cluster around port cities. Once we pointed away from Trisse and into the bay, we were safe."

She shook her head. Why did she worry so much when no one else did?

After a quick midday meal at a small inn, Rapunzel and her mother loaded little Helena into a fine hired carriage as the men and servants loaded a supply wagon. The king had made arrangements to have them waiting at the small inn.

When all were settled, the driver climbed atop the carriage. Paul, Jacob, and Amis rode in front, with several armed knights behind. Horses for Katterina and Rapunzel were tied behind the supply wagon. They set off at the mouth of the Auriel River and began their journey following it, knowing it would soon lead them to the Dark Wood.

SIBLINGS AND SQUABBLES

Sometimes Gwynndolen wished she were a man, but this was not one of those times. As she came to her brothers' bedchambers, she stood outside their door, listening to Liam talk about how he would "catch" a lady at court that summer and win a prize against the other lords and princes in the tournament.

A fair-haired young maid came down the hallway carrying a pitcher of wine and several glasses. "Is that for my brothers?"

The dark-eyed girl nodded but said nothing. "Here, I will take it to them."

"Thank you, milady," the shy maidservant whispered, as though afraid of their boisterous shouts.

"Liam! Liam will—"

The stench that struck her as she opened the door made her eyes water. Didn't they ever bathe? Or change their clothes? The only maid they could catch would be one who couldn't smell. "Hold on!" Gwynndolen nearly shouted above the ruckus. "We leave on the morrow and you're shouting in here?"

"We thought we'd go down to the alehouse soon. Why don't you join us, sweet sister? Perhaps someone there will catch your fancy and you can wallop him?"

Gwynndolen rolled her eyes. She had learned long ago that when her brothers were rowdy, there was no point in arguing. They would have their say, and that was that. She set down the tray and got out of their way. She pitied the maid who had to clean up after them.

She wandered around the castle aimlessly and found her way outside and to the stables. This was where she felt safest, where she felt she had a sense of purpose. Tomorrow she and her siblings—well, all of them that were old enough, the little ones were still home with her mother and father— would set sail. She should celebrate, be excited. But instead, fear and a sense of dread lingered as she waited. She would set sail on the morrow. And how was she spending the evening before? Just waiting.

Why was she so different? Could it be because her blood wasn't that of a noble-born woman? Though, she had to admit, she didn't really want to be a man; she enjoyed being and thinking like a woman. But she hated that she sometimes felt tied up by the expectations of others—expectations only noble families had. What if she had been given to a common family when she was orphaned as an infant? Her whole life would have taken a different turn. Gwynndolen snorted at the thought that she certainly wouldn't have had to worry about High Court. She imagined everyone there would be much like Beatrix: scheming, backbiting. But her sister hadn't always been that way. How long had it been since the two of them had been good friends? So long that her mind struggled to remember.

"I thought I might find you here, sister." She flinched when she heard Beatrix's strident tone.

"And so you have." Gwynndolen looked at her sister in

amusement as she hesitated to come any nearer to the horses than the entrance of the stables.

"Why aren't you with the queen this evening?"

Gwynndolen shrugged her shoulders and picked up a brush, though her mare didn't really need brushing again.

"You should come back to the castle and ready yourself."

"For what?"

"The journey ahead. You won't know anything about anyone if you don't start paying attention. There are some very important people who—"

"Oh, Beatrix, don't you ever long to be out and away?"

"Out and away? From what?"

"The expectations of others. The demands. The—the —" But her tongue failed her. She couldn't make it say what she wanted to say, and she couldn't think. It was apparent by the look on her sister's face that Beatrix couldn't understand Gwynndolen's frustrations.

"I enjoy being inside, I enjoy being seen."

"I know you do."

"And I enjoy going to court. It's why I will make some lord—or king!—a wonderful wife. I know and understand how to do and say the right things. I work at it, and it is a credit to our family. *And* I don't smell like a horse."

"My work with our horses has been a credit to our family. Maybe if you came riding—"

"I get so weary of all the talk of horses!"

"I wasn't trying to say you had to be like me, Beatrix, I just don't understand how you—"

"You think you're better because you can teach the prince, because you can help him. Do you really think he will want to marry someone who thinks she's better than he is? Just remember, you didn't have a noble family till we took you in!"

Beatrix enjoyed bringing up Gwynndolen's adoption

when it suited her, but Gwynndolen refused to address it. Lady Genevieve had long ago told her how much they loved her, and that even if her birth had been common, her upbringing had taught her to not lower herself to such arguments. Still, she couldn't resist correcting Beatrix on one point.

"I didn't say I was better than the prince, and I *never* said he wanted to marry—"

"It doesn't really matter, anyway!" Beatrix stopped her. "I could have had him if I wanted, but I'll find a better match."

Gwynndolen stopped brushing her mare's mane and stared. "A better match than the future king of Rona?"

"I think a king of Alleria will be much more to my liking. Getting off this island will get me closer to the High Court."

"And that's what you want?"

"It's all I've ever wanted."

Gwynndolen stared at her sister and thought of all the time she spent preening and practicing proper etiquette. That was the life her sister wanted. She wasn't a horrible person, but she was small in Gwynndolen's eyes. "Then I wish you well"—she didn't stop her words from pouring out —"and I hope my smell doesn't deter your future suitors."

"Oh, don't worry, I won't let anyone know we are sisters."

"Then, why bother talking to me now?"

"I don't know!" Her sister turned on her heel and flew back to the castle.

Gwynndolen rested her forehead against the rough mane of her mare and sighed. It would be an endless journey across the sea.

THE CALLING OF A FOOL

It wasn't that Amis had wanted to leave the Fisher King behind, but he knew better than to ignore the calling of God. There were things ahead that Jacob was not prepared for, and Amis was happy to help along the way. Amis and the warrior monk had tried to sup with the knights at mealtime, but Prince Paul had asked him to sit with the family around their fire for the duration of the journey. It was an honor that the fool wanted to pay back by looking after the family well.

After a needed day of rest, the men went to hunt on the edge of the Wood. They would travel beside the Auriel into it on the morrow, but first Paul wanted a day to find good eating while giving the women an excuse for one more day of rest. Paul asked that Amis attend to the womenfolk while the rest went to hunt. Amis nodded, determined that he could find more ways to be helpful than merely keeping watch.

"Lady Katterina," he began, loping alongside her as she walked around the camp, "what shall we do with ourselves today?"

The lady took in a long breath. "I'm uncertain, silly fool. I think the prince has forgotten that the princess and myself do not need coddling. We were the ones who journeyed with him to defeat Ute. Why these two days of rest at the beginning of our journey? We're not weary yet! And we are riding in a carriage instead of on the backs of horses up a mountain in pursuit of a sorceress."

A squeal split the morning air, and Amis laughed. "I doubt very much that the prince is trying to coddle you. I think it has more to do with the babe."

Katterina's face broke into a smile. "She has become quite a handful since we started traveling. I suppose for her sake I can forgive the prince this indulgence."

Amis chuckled at her concession. "And don't forget, the prince needs his excuse to hunt. I don't think he can go more than a fortnight without doing so these days."

"Are you speaking of my husband?" Rapunzel poked her head out of a dark blue tent, and Helena giggled and reached for Amis. He grabbed the tyke and threw her up in the air, making her laugh even harder.

"We were just saying that we noticed how Prince Paul needs more time to hunt lately than ever before."

"Well, I think he uses it to sharpen his training skills. It will bolster his confidence when competing in the tournaments."

"He will do well."

Rapunzel nodded, but a flicker of a frown crossed her face. Amis was not one to pretend he didn't notice.

"Princess," he said, kneeling to the ground and letting little Helena play on the scrub of grass, "you worry too much."

Rapunzel's emerald eyes blinked back tears. "I don't want this trip. It will be so hard to let her go."

Katterina placed a hand on her daughter's shoulder. Few

women, in Amis's experience, knew when to stay quiet. Katterina did. There was nothing they could say to relieve the burden the princess carried. There was no trick he could do to lighten the load. At times, he really felt like a fool.

ONE WOULD THINK BEING a huge leviathan would cause many difficulties when coming near to the docks, but now that her powers had grown, it was easy for Camilla to reach into the thoughts of the workers. Here they were, readying the king's ship to set sail at the break of dawn. The sun was peering over the horizon to the east, as though it, too, were spying on the workers. Brilliant oranges and yellows and pinks flooded the cloud-free sky. The workers didn't note the beauty, but Camilla did. She coveted it. The sorceress wanted it for her own. She would soon *be* east, at last! It would be simple to find her little sister and take back what was rightfully theirs. Her heart skipped a beat when thinking of how Ute's death had stalled their progress. Still, they would be together again soon, and it would only take a little nudging on this trip to get Prince Edmund to do exactly as she needed.

Camilla dove beneath the waters with glee, looking around her with eyes that could pierce through the underwater darkness. She reached out, trying to see how much further she could now travel, but she could not reach as far as she liked. But with the little prince leading the way, it would change soon. The leviathan laughed to herself, bubbles of mirth floating to the surface.

THE DARK WOOD

The Wood was as dark as Rapunzel remembered. The trees were thick with leaves as though it were summer and not early spring. Katterina had insisted Rapunzel take a turn riding into the Wood next to Paul. They had been traveling a full two days into the forest, and it staggered belief that the Wood continued to grow ever darker. She glanced behind at the carriage. Would Helena sleep for Katterina instead of fussing like she had the day before?

The sound of the leaves was just as she remembered. Rustles caused a whispering, a whispering that preyed on her fears. She looked over at Paul—could he hear it? If so, he gave no sign. As though sensing her distress, he turned and looked at her, dappled light gliding over his features as the horses walked along.

"Rapunzel?" He inclined his head, his hazel eyes more golden today, creased in concern.

"I've been here before."

"Yes, the Dark Wood was where you met that woman . . ."

"Dorothea."

"She helped you, right?"

"Yes. I had almost given up. I was so tired of my witch's tricks, so sad thinking you were dead. God put Dorothea right in my way so I had to find her, so I would let go of false hope and live with genuine hope instead. She told me—" Her voice broke with a little laugh. "She told me the funniest stories of others who came her way. The women always wept too much, but eventually Dorothea would help them find their way. And learn to stop crying so much.

"I've met many in the service of God, but none like Dorothea . . ." Her voice trailed off as she looked over at her husband. How was it that there was a trail wide enough for them to ride side by side? She knew the location of the Dark Wood and how the road beside the Auriel was a connection from the Northlands into Alleria, but when she had been here before it had seemed isolated, untraveled.

"How large is the Dark Wood?"

Paul's laughter dispelled some of her anxiety. "Oh Rapunzel, the Dark Wood is massive. It stretches across most of Alleria, with clearings in several spots like the hill country or the Tippoli Mountains where the Winter Castle of the High King rests. It is only here on the northern side that so many people complain of its darkness and propensity toward magic."

Rapunzel's mind whirled. Had she been in the Wood several times and just not realized it? She thought of all the different misadventures she had in Alleria during her first year of freedom beyond the tower. Had she been entering and exiting the same wood over and over, never knowing it till it became darkest of all?

"Are you speaking of the Dark Wood?" Rapunzel had been so deep in her own thoughts she hadn't noticed the crunching leaves as Amis rode up close behind them.

Paul nodded. "It is where we are."

"Yes, and there are so many fantastic stories about it, especially this part. Isn't this where you got caught, Rapunzel? I do so hope to meet with some terrific adventure while we are here."

"I hope we don't! We have Helena with us—I want her safe."

"Oh, well, safe adventures are scarce. And I don't really think that's what God has for us."

Amis dropped back before Rapunzel could ask him what he meant by that, but when she looked over her shoulder, she could see the silly grin on his face as he raised those dark eyebrows up high, close to his jester's hat. Good grief, the man was always vexing her or causing her to laugh at herself.

"To tell you the truth, Rapunzel," Paul said, his horse now closer to her, "I have only been this way a few times on my way to the Eastern Ports."

Rapunzel forced a smile on her face as she spoke. "And you had no misadventures?"

"No, not even when we crossed the Auriel. And the hunting was good. I think the darkness in this part provides a haven for all sorts of creatures."

Oh, how she wished Paul hadn't said "creatures"! She thought of the phantoms she had met and wondered if she had imagined such terrors. But no, her mother had confirmed that good and evil were lurking here. She did not relish the idea of encountering the latter.

Rapunzel glanced behind her to where the carriage was following on the wide trail. Perhaps she should have stayed in the carriage to protect Helena. But what protection could she provide the little one? She was just a woman who wished she could hold on to a child not even her own.

The dark days stretched on as they continued through the Wood. Rapunzel alternated with her mother so they each had a break from being cloistered in the carriage with a cranky baby.

SETTING SAIL

The brisk air hit Edmund in the face as the carriage clattered quickly to the docks. He breathed in the smell of salt while watching out the open window as sailors scurried to ready the ship. Though he had visited Maer the summer before, Edmund had never been on a ship. He knew the white rectangles of material would catch the wind, and that would propel them through the waters, but it wasn't the mechanics of the voyage that worried him. Now that he knew what lurked beneath the waters, he feared he was drawing the entire ship into danger.

He couldn't take back all the things he had wished, could he? If only it worked that way! What sort of king would he be to endanger the lives of the crew and passengers? But Camilla needed him alive. And he could use that to his advantage, couldn't he?

All at once, Edmund heard his name. The king was talking to him. How long had he been speaking? They had taken a separate carriage from the queen, and Edmund now realized it was so that the king could have time alone to instruct his heir. Another missed opportunity to serve his father well. He felt like an idiot.

"Edmund?" King Purnell's thin lips were firm, as always, and those dark Ronan eyes pierced through Edmund as though to make sense of why the prince hadn't been paying attention.

"I'm sorry, Father, I've never been aboard. I was lost in my own thoughts."

"Well," the king said as he cleared his throat and nodded, "we suppose that's understandable. But we will need you to be very aware of your actions over the next few months. People will look to you to see what we think of things. Especially once we reach the Eastern Ports. You will represent our entire kingdom, and you know that there are—"

"Yes, Father, you have explained that there are those looking for weaknesses. We will not show any. You have the largest kingdom under the High King because you are such an able king. We will make certain to make the best of things this summer."

"And with all the help you've received, we know you'll do well representing Rona at the tournament."

Edmund felt his lips smile even as he swallowed hard when the carriage came to a stop. He knew there were those who could fight to the death to defend their kingdoms without a bit of concentration. He would be lucky to not fall off his horse. His eyes followed a movement to the right as the carriage stopped. Gwynndolen was directing workers as they were bringing the horses on board. They blindfolded the horses to keep them from being spooked. A dozen of the muscular animals were ready for the High King, and a few others had been brought along as personal mounts for King Purnell's company.

He felt crammed aboard with people and animals. For a moment, he longed for the time when he had only to speak a wish to carry himself over the waters. But now that he knew each wish was granting power to Camilla, he couldn't let himself do it again.

As he walked up the gangplank to board, the water shifted under the boat and he felt the little bridge move. Startled by the swaying, he was grateful as Georgius caught his hand and pulled him onboard.

"Gotcha!" the good-natured man laughed, thumping him on the back.

Edmund was glad to see him. He pushed away darker thoughts.

"First time on a ship?"

"Yes," Edmund said, glancing about.

"Don't worry about that, you'll get your sea legs soon enough."

But Edmund wasn't sure. His feet seemed unsure of where to step, and his balance teetered as they all went belowdecks to find their cabins by way of a claustrophobic corridor. Each room seemed to be just a nook with several beds stacked on top of one another, with only enough space to climb in and shut the door. Not that he hadn't been in small places before, but when he was a troubadour, he had just elected to sleep outside. Now he was crowded by the other young lords and constantly followed by his manservant, Blanc. At least the man was quiet and kept to himself.

Georgius pointed out which bunk was his, and then they climbed up the steep stairs to the upper decks just in time to see the queen come aboard. Edmund trusted the cabin for the king and queen would be better than his own.

His mother looked lovely, as always, smile lines deepening as she looked around her. Edmund smiled at them, watching as the king guided the queen with his arm wrapped around her for support. But—he hesitated, his own smile fading— who was his father, really? A man who had allowed so much tragedy in their family. A man who had vowed to wed and care for Queen Lefwenna and then left her to her own devices. Devices that had led her to attempt suicide and drown her only child's hope of a normal life.

But she had forgiven him, and here they were, reconciled. Now Edmund was paying the price for the king's mistakes. He felt as though someone had left him out in the cold—but he couldn't blame everything on his father or his mother. He had made his own horrible choices too.

Once the entire party was on board, the sailors raised the sails. Edmund stared as the wind blew into them. The ship began its swim across the Illyan Sea, sailing faster than Edmund had imagined possible.

AFTER SEVERAL DAYS OF TRAVEL, both Katterina and Rapunzel were in the carriage together, trying to settle Helena down. Katterina's feline impatience reasserted itself. "She won't break," she said, plucking Helena from Rapunzel's arms and plopping her onto the carriage floor. The babe started scooting toward the door, but Katterina rerouted her. They repeated this over and over, but when Rapunzel tried to "rescue" Helena, Katterina was just as firm, saying, "No, watch."

She dangled her leather pouch before the crabby Helena, and the baby instantly grabbed at it, beginning to gum and slobber all over it. "Mm-hmm, she's probably teething."

Katterina was glad for the way her eyes worked. She still saw through the dark better than most humans, though she had never felt the need to tell her daughter this. Even in the gloom, she could see that Rapunzel was distressed. "I suppose I probably should have said something, Rapunzel, but I thought it was obvious. She's been drooling for weeks and chewing on my fingers when I hold her."

"She's been doing that for a while with me. That means she is teething?"

Katterina nodded, but then gave a soft grunt of assent when she realized her daughter could barely see her. Rapunzel continued to stare through the darkness at her. Did she feel the way Katterina felt, that they just didn't know each other or how to deal with one another? Katterina adored Rapunzel, but it was odd finally being together. To be truthful, even after all these months, it was still odd to be human again.

"So," Rapunzel began in what seemed a tolerant tone, "what we can do with our little Helena?"

Katterina frowned before answering. "Well, we just give her something to gum on so she can chew on it, drool on it, and she'll break the tooth through her gums soon enough."

"We give her 'something'?"

"Well, not just anything! I wouldn't hand her a knife or something sharp, but tough leather is good. In the winter, a bit of snow can numb the mouth."

"But it's not winter now, Mother."

"No, I suppose not." Katterina shrugged, suddenly wishing she had the power to change the season for her grandchild—Helga's child. "I guess it can't be helped. We'll just make do with a bit of ale or wine on the gums next time we stop. But not too much!"

Silence eluded them once more when Helena grew weary of chewing and cried. The women took turns for the rest of the day trying to distract her.

The horses were handling the trip remarkably well, proving again to Gwynndolen how much they trusted her to care for them. Though the smell of livestock and manure could be oppressive as she visited them in the bowels of the ship, she enjoyed her morning duties. She loved bringing them fresh water and hay with Georgius each morning after their own quick bite. Forgoing breaking fast with the women, especially Beatrix, was all right with her. One by one, she and Georgius would visit each of the horses, taking time to talk, touch them, to remind them they were safe. The horses grew calm, even though the ground beneath their feet was moving and liked to tip from side to side. Gwynndolen was grateful that they would stop at several little islands dotting the way to the Eastern Ports. The horses needed fresh air and a good ride.

"It's good the weather has been fair. I remember your first trip . . ." Georgius's voice trailed off and Gwynndolen had to laugh.

"Well, I was young and didn't know!"

"You had been told, but you thought you knew best."

She shook her head. "I hope I never make such a mistake again."

"What happened?"

Gwynndolen turned from the horse she was patting, surprised to see the prince had descended.

"Well, our sweet Gwynndolen got restless on the way to court. She was certain the horses weren't getting enough exercise, so she removed the sling from around her favorite mare and walked her around."

Edmund stared at the slings wrapped around each horse, helping them to stay upright even if the ship was swaying. Then the prince glanced about, his tilted smile forming. The base of the ship was not large, by any estimation. "While the ship was still sailing?"

"Yes," Gwynndolen admitted, feeling her face heat. The ship dipped slightly to the right, but though the horses whinnied and pawed the ground a little, their slings kept them steady. The tension in the hold eased the instant the brother and sister spoke in soothing tones. "You're fine," Gwynndolen said, rubbing the velvety nose of the stallion, and she laughed when he curled back his lips as though expecting a treat. "Yes, yes, you'll get something soon!"

Edmund wasn't as easily distracted as the horses, though. "What went wrong?"

"It's as you guessed—there's a reason we keep them in slings. Gwynndolen was lucky she didn't end up under the mare. I came down about that time—"

"Luckily for me!"

"—and then we began the hard job of trying to get the mare back on her feet and in the sling while the ship was pitching. The other horses were—well, to say it upset them would be an understatement."

"I've never had so many bruises in all my life."

"Nor I!"

"And the mess! Everything was everywhere! Muck covered us for most of that trip, if I remember right."

"First time I was happy to finish and see the horses gone."

"We lost two," Gwynndolen stated, her throat tight with regret.

Georgius nodded soberly. "It was a hard lesson learned."

Gwynndolen glanced up at Edmund, wondering what he was thinking with that frown on his face. "So, um, how do you get rid of the—muck?—while onboard?"

His sideways smile made her wonder who he was: a difficult, melancholy prince, or a fun-spirited troubadour? "Well, we don't save it, there's no room for that while sailing. We pitch it overboard every day."

"And whose job is that?"

Now she laughed. "Whoever is watching the horse collects it, but Liam has to pitch it. We drew lots before we left home."

"Poor Liam," was all Edmund said while his smile finished stretching across his face.

"Oh, if you feel that badly for him, I'm sure we could work something out, Your Highness. He could let you do it for him today."

Edmund held up his hands in mock seriousness. "You know, I think my father wanted me to speak with him this morning. I'll see the two of you later." And he was up the stairs that quickly.

A FOOL'S ADVENTURE

Though the heavy darkness collected beneath the trees, the cheery fool's sense of adventure beckoned him forward. The future was undefined; it was more of a moving shape with a few defined corners. It was best described as a moving shadow that he sometimes got a glimpse of, Lord willing. And this trip—well, he was glad no one had asked him about this trip. He didn't know what he could reply if they asked.

Amis shifted in his saddle, trusting his horse to follow Paul and Rapunzel as they continued deeper and deeper into the Wood. He prayed for insight. There, in his mind's eye, he could see two swiftly moving groups of adventurers journeying to meet at a destination that would divide them all. No specifics, nothing normal mortals could understand. He chuckled to himself. A fool should never explain until the adventure concluded. Then and only then could he weave it into a song or story to be told before a warm fire.

Glancing up after his reverie, Amis noted Rapunzel's shoulders were nearly up to her ears. He clicked his tongue and trotted up close to the couple. "Something amiss?"

Paul looked over his shoulder. "It's this wood and our journey—they have Princess Rapunzel worried."

Amis made a noise that he hoped sounded comforting. "I think we need to find a place to rest for a day or so."

"I wish we could just be done with this darkness!" Rapunzel grumbled.

"Ah! Sweet princess, it's in the darkness we see the need for the light."

She looked over her shoulder now, and the look she gave him should have made him shut his mouth, but instead he laughed. "Dorothea's just ahead."

"She's—who's—what?"

"Look!" He pointed ahead, and among the trees it suddenly became clear that a cozy cottage, entwined by vines, was waiting for them. The door opened, and a little old woman ventured forth, light spilling out all around her. Amis laughed, his chest growing warm at the thought of the fellowship ahead. It was just as he had seen. Here she was, ready to welcome and refresh them. A brown-skinned boy— a lanky young man, really—popped out next to her, holding to the old woman's arm as though a strong wind might whisk her away.

Rapunzel was off her mount at once and running to Dorothea, but she stopped just in front of her and halted in awkward silence until the woman tottered forward with her arms stretched out. Rapunzel fell into them at once with a happy cry.

It didn't take long for the party to find a stream to water the horses, hobbling them nearby. Before evening was fully upon them, they all made their way inside, and Amis laughed at how Rapunzel's mouth dropped open when everyone, even the knights, fit within.

Katterina patted her daughter on the shoulder as she

laughed. "The God of heaven made this house accommo-date any who need it, right, Rapunzel?"

"Oh! I just never thought—" But she didn't have time to complete her thought. In front of them were set bowls of savory, hearty stew, fresh bread, and heavy tankards of frothy ale, making Amis's mouth water. Dorothea gave even baby Helena some gruel, and time passed quickly as mouths munched.

Dorothea and the young man were soon escorting the knights to the many rooms, but Amis knew his adventure-some group needed time to sit before the hearth. He had noted the strange whorl tattoo on the boy's jaw and knew there was a story here. Amis practically smacked his lips. He had been looking forward to this and wanted to know all about the Dark Wood. At last, this was where he could learn of its history!

Rapunzel and Katterina chattered as they cleaned up. Dorothea laughed when she returned from making the knights comfortable. "Here I come to do my chores, and you have already taken care of it. You don't make well-behaved guests, my dears!" She sat down in a worn rocking chair while the young man, Dietz, huddled by the fire, his skinny legs pulled up to his chest.

Rapunzel looked over at Paul with mischief twinkling in her eyes. "I suppose I won't make a very good queen, then."

"A queen?" The woman only looked slightly surprised as her eyes fell instantly on Paul. "Is this your beloved?"

"And husband."

"But—you said he had died."

"Yes, I thought he had. My witch had led me to believe that, but really, she had stolen his memory and sent him to Rona to keep us apart. She thought I would mourn him and not be able to move forward."

The old woman's eyes nearly disappeared as her smile crowded wrinkles around them. "But you found your way, didn't you?"

"Well, I needed your help to do so."

"And perhaps the help of a cat? Katterina—" Dorothea's voice bubbled when she turned to look at the woman. "I never thought to see you in your human form. What has freed you of your curse?"

Katterina lifted a shoulder. "I have received a grace I never deserved."

"None of us deserves grace. That's what makes it so miraculous. Now come, sit, and introduce me to this new family of yours."

Amis had had enough of listening and he bound forward, bouncing on his toes. "Oh, please, let me do the introductions. I think I know the tale well enough to help Dorothea!"

Dorothea let out a merry laugh, and as she sat with a sigh in her well-worn rocker, Amis sang. He gestured first to the women, reminding the group of how Rapunzel and Katterina became estranged when the mother chose fear and greed and betrayed her sister and witch, Eufemia. Transformed into a cat, Katterina had wandered the kingdom, spying for the witch and Ute, the sorceress whose curse had kept her tied to the mountain. Amis hopped over to Paul and told of his enchantment. The witch had stolen Paul's memory of Rapunzel until the maid cried and kissed him, breaking the spell and defeating the witch. Though Katterina had tried to forgive the witch, Eufemia's bitterness had caused her frozen heart to shatter within her. Amis then bowed and sang of how he had met Rapunzel only the summer before at Lord Col's castle in Maer, but he had known that he would have to help her. So he left Lord Col and crossed the Illyan Sea to return to the Fisher King's realm and service. When Paul and Rapunzel arrived at the Fisher King's court, he surprised them. With the help of the warrior monk Jacob, the small group had set out to defeat Ute and keep her from reuniting the sisters of sorcery. His voice rose in triumph as he sang of Ute's demise and the freeing of the children who had been sapped of their strength.

"And you returned to the Fisher King's court with the little baby?" Dorothea asked, turning her eyes on Rapunzel.

"Yes, our poor little Helena." Rapunzel was rubbing slow little circles on the girl's back as she held the sleeping babe close. "We had planned to send for her family, but now we will find them ourselves, since we must go to the Eastern Ports."

Amis liked the way Dorothea kept nodding with a small smile on her lips, as though all this had been expected. "I see." The woman reached over and patted the thin shoulder of the young man. "This explains much to us, doesn't it, Dietz?"

He nodded, his dark brown eyes suddenly shadowed. "Beware. All should fear who head to the Eastern Ports. There are others from our coven—"

"Your *what*?" Amis had heard Jacob's voice sound like that before. The young man should take care.

"Those who despise the God of heaven raised Dietz." Dorothea frowned, stilling in her rocking chair. "But he ran away when it all fell apart. Last winter he came to me, shivering, silent. Alone. And I was alone, too. I had just hurt my back after a fall, and I'm not sure what I would have done without him. He got over his silence once he warmed up. He has been learning about God's goodness and provision ever since, much as you did, my Rapunzel."

The pink hue that flushed Rapunzel's cheeks also heightened the green of her eyes.

Dietz screwed his mouth into a tight scowl. "My people —but they aren't really my people anymore—many of them were going to the Eastern Ports. To meet up with another coven there. The bond had snapped."

"What bond?" Paul frowned.

"The bond from the witch, Eufemia, and also from Ute. It was weak, then became strong, then snapped." He shrugged. "My—the people went to the Eastern Ports. To find out why."

"Eufemia's death, Ute's death—this must be why." Dorothea's rocking resumed, a quiet creak returning a rhythm to their discussion. "Dietz's coven knew nothing of what catastrophe had taken place, so they had to go get their orders in person to know when the invasion was to begin."

Paul straightened at this. "What invasion?"

Dietz eyes darted around the room. "It is time for the war. Many have infiltrated the church, covens planted all over the land—but without Eufemia the witch connecting us to Ute . . . One group went to the Eastern Ports. Another stayed behind. Supposed to keep the darkness here. It was my adopted brothers and myself, but I ran away." The young man tried to take a breath before continuing, hugging his knees hard to his chest, but his halting speech continued to pour out, strained. "It terrified me. It was wrong, what we were doing. Took off. Didn't know where I was going. So hungry. Then Dorothea opened her door." He shrugged again, his eyebrows drawn together.

Rapunzel nodded with understanding. "Those who are meant to find Dorothea do. I'm glad you did."

There was a hesitant pause that crept into the air, and they all looked at one another expectantly. What was next? Amis looked on the company with a hungry air of impatience. At last, a new thread of the story was entwined with the old one. Yes, it was leading them closer and closer to their destination, the great divide at the Eastern Ports.

"We'll have more time in the morning," the old woman said into the unsettled silence. "Let us show you to your rooms." Well, Amis sighed, he'd just have to wait a little longer. But, anticipation made any story sweeter, didn't it?

HORSES AND PURPOSE

Gwynndolen made her way topside after feeding the horses. Beatrix was looking out over the sea at the starboard bow. There was nothing but endless cobalt from horizon to horizon. Beatrix had covered her hair, which was unusual for a Ronan maid, but she complained that if she didn't, the wind made a tangled mess of her long brown locks. Her sister wrinkled her nose as she approached. "Gwynndolen, why must you always smell?"

"Because, dear sister, I work hard."

"Hard work is for men. We are ladies, meant to take our leisure and—"

Liam and Georgius joined them at the ship's bow. Gwynndolen laughed as her sister wrinkled her nose even more at the aroma her brothers brought up with them. She glanced around, noticing sailors all over the deck conducting several different tasks to keep the ship running. The captain's tan, weathered face kept scowling at them. He didn't like having so many aboard and walking on the deck, but she didn't care. It was important to enjoy the voyage. What if she never made this journey again? Never again with this group of siblings together.

It was a strange thing to think of. When they returned at the end of summer, Beatrix would likely be betrothed, and Georgius would marry his sweetheart, Fressenda. Perhaps even Liam would find a wife who could stand his stench. The only reason none of them had married yet was because of their father's ill health for so many years. So much had stalled in their family because of his illness. It had stopped them from normalcy, but it had also strengthened them. She would not have enjoyed as much time with her brothers had they gone to train under different lords around Rona. But now, they would find their own places, and Gwynndolen needed to consider her own state of affairs.

"Are you ladies looking for fish?" Liam asked, knowing it would irritate Beatrix.

"Of course not! A lady doesn't fish."

"Gwynndolen might."

She laughed. "No! I have no desire to fish, myself."

"Besides," Beatrix jumped in, "one can hardly think of Gwynndolen as a *lady*."

"I wouldn't say that. I would say that Gwynndolen isn't *only* a lady."

Beatrix tossed her head, her eyes flashing. "And what would you call me?"

"Only a lady!" Liam elbowed her, but she didn't find it funny.

"I have qualities none of you appreciate! But you'd be lucky to find a lady as fine as me to wed." She stomped off below.

Georgius gave Liam a look.

"What? She needed talking down . . . Fine!" He turned to go.

"And hurry back, the prince will be up soon."

Gwynndolen watched him go, shielding her eyes with her hand from the sun's glare. "If he doesn't return soon enough, I can help this morning."

"You wouldn't mind crossing swords with the prince? I'd never have guessed."

Gwynndolen shot him a smile. She'd always liked, not just loved, Georgius, even if he was teasing her. Like his father, he had a firm jaw, now somewhat stubbled with the growth of a red beard that refused to match his dark hair and brows. His mouth, often smiling, had the thin lips of their father, which could be stern when he was training. Unlike most of her brothers and her difficult older sister, he seemed to understand her best. Most of the time. He put an arm around her, as though he knew something was wrong.

"You look too deep in thought, sister. What troubles you?"

"This may be our last trip together, all of us brothers and sisters."

"Ha! I'd not thought of that. I suppose you're right. Some of us may not return for long, depending on how the tournament goes—and if Beatrix finds someone at court!" His eyes lit in silent laughter.

Gwynndolen leaned into his side while she stared ahead at the sparkles the high sun cast on the waters. She thought of how careful Georgius had been in selecting his bride. As the eldest of their father's sons, he would inherit the castle and responsibility of caring for the serfs. Fressenda was a woman who would shoulder the duties of being a lady well. She wasn't a gossip, but a hard worker, caring and compassionate for those beneath her. She spent time both at her needle and outdoors. Yes, she would be a wonderful lady to take over the fiefdom, but would such a woman mind if Gwynndolen stayed on beneath her brother's protection, should she choose not to marry?

She pulled away so she could look her brother in the face. "If I don't, um, make a match, will you and Fressenda send me away?"

"Where?"

"To a convent?"

"Why would I do that? I doubt the nuns would want you." He laughed, and then stopped when Gwynndolen didn't join in. "You're serious? Sister, if you can't make a good match, I'd rather you stayed on to keep training the horses. I wasn't lying when I told Prince Edmund you were invaluable."

Gwynndolen looked down at the mention of the prince. She didn't want to think of him, or the match his mother had proposed.

"What's wrong?"

"Nothing."

Georgius took her by the shoulders and waited till she looked up at him. "I think you will find a match, a good one, a man who will understand you and not make you preen and float about gossiping and sewing all day. Father's not able to be here, so our mother gave me leave to look out for you and Beatrix. I'll not match you with anyone who doesn't understand who you are or what you're best at."

Gwynndolen sucked in a deep breath. She hadn't realized how much she needed to hear that. "I know courtly life is necessary—" But here she faltered.

"Oh, that it is, but no one will dictate to you about your conduct at court. You don't have to make it miserable, find a way to enjoy it! Besides, I imagine old friends will be there."

"Really? Who?"

"There is a tale that your friend is now a princess, heir to the Fisher King's throne. I forgot how helpful it is to travel to Maer to catch up on the latest news."

"Soon we will have our fill of such news," Gwynndolen

groaned, thinking of the hours ahead, listening to women prattle on, their needles pricking in and out of cloth, weaving designs that bored her. "Still, I am so glad to hear of Rapun—*Princess* Rapunzel."

"I thought you would be, though our prince may not be. Well, here he comes."

Gwynndolen frowned as she saw Edmund approach. She had not thought of his meeting Rapunzel. Indeed! Perhaps this would prove to be a very interesting season at court after all.

FIGHTING

*E*dmund could feel someone staring at him while he practiced his swordplay with Georgius and Liam. He looked away, only to find that the brothers used the movement to their advantage. "And that moment of distraction would have you run through if I were a different man." The oldest brother frowned, his blade pointed squarely at Edmund's chest. Edmund was glad of the man's help, but sometimes he hated that someone younger than himself, even if just barely, knew so much more than he did.

"It's hard for him to concentrate, so long as Gwynndolen is staring at him." Liam laughed.

"I don't mean to be a distraction, but with the two of you against one of him, he will not win. Unless . . ."

"Unless what, My Lady?" Edmund tried to temper his voice with deference, as was due her station. But she walked over to him, eyes bright with mischief, and he wondered what trouble he was in for.

She lunged, striking fast at Liam's belly with a short sword she had concealed among her skirts. "Make your weakness your advantage when they underestimate you!"

Liam parried, just barely in time, and he advanced on her, but she side-stepped, using how he lunged low to adjust for her lack of height, and tripped him. When he fell, she touched the tip of her short sword to his exposed neck. "Just like this, Your Highness!" And her laughter filled the air. Even the sailors stopped their work to look at the young woman with the flaming hair.

"I'd say you were the one with the advantage, My Lady," Edmund said, re-sheathing his sword and wiping the back of his sweaty neck. "Although, I thought that sword would be too short to be any good."

"See, you're underestimating me. The short sword allows me to be flexible and maneuverable. No, my brothers always have the upper hand in might. Liam didn't notice I had gone for my sword, and he often forgets how good I am at nimble footwork, right?"

Liam stood up, laughing good-naturedly and brushing himself off. "It's true. I should always observe her."

"Georgius rarely falls for my ploys, but every once in a while . . ."

Georgius grinned in agreement.

"Only then can I use their strength against them."

Edmund clapped for her, and she gave a small curtsy, which made him laugh. How many more surprises did this maid have in store for him?

⁂

KATTERINA CLOSED the door as quietly as possible, wincing at the rustle of her clothing as she padded her way down the hall. There, dozing before the burning embers, sat Dorothea in her rocker, a worn quilt snugged around her lap. Katterina sat herself at the hearth, enjoying the last bit of warmth. She watched the woman breathe in deeply and wondered again how old she was. The wrinkled woman's face frowned in sleep and then she sat up, awake. "Oh, Cat!" She sputtered a laugh before reaching to light a candle. "You startled me!"

"Did I?"

"You've always been good at surprising me. I wonder, were you like that when you were a girl, before you were feline?"

"No, not at all." Katterina felt her mouth stretch into a smile. "I think it came with becoming Cat, and hasn't faded now that I am"—she gestured to herself—"what I am. Why are you sleeping out here?"

"Oh, these old bones, I can't ever settle them in bed anymore. I prefer to sit here and rock myself to sleep. Isn't it funny that what we needed when we were wee babes we need again as we grow older?"

Katterina didn't like the sound of that, but Dorothea just smiled at her.

"It's all as it should be, my dear, my time is coming. I see it before me. I've been in this Wood for ages, and in here it has only grown darker and darker. It's time for someone else to bring the light here."

"Are you—are you dying?" She didn't like to speak the words, but if she could find out what was wrong, then she could try to mend Dorothea. Rapunzel didn't *really* need her in the Eastern Ports. Truth told, she'd much prefer being home, helping the apothecary heal the sick. Katterina could easily stay behind to nurse her old friend back to health.

The old woman gave a chuckle. "You have a cure for old age? There's nothing wrong with me, I've simply lived long enough. Visitors have become fewer and fewer, and now that Ysentrude has found her way home at last, there's little for me left to do."

Katterina sat up tall. Memories of Dorothea's ghoulish daughter who had locked herself away in mourning, living on only as some living ghost, flashed through her mind. "Ysentrude is free?"

The old woman nodded, a sad smile lifting the corners of her mouth. Her words were slow as she explained, "Late last winter, my daughter called to me. You know I almost never went into her room of mourning. She was so thin, and most of her lustrous hair had fallen out. But something had changed—her warbling song of sorrow had finished and she asked me to pray for her. She wanted to lay it down."

"Why then?"

"I had had an adventure of my own. When Dietz came to live with me, he discovered Nicolas. You knew about him, didn't you?"

Katterina frowned, but nodded. "Whenever I tried to warn you how he inhabited your room of sorting dreams, Eufemia would take my voice away. I hated knowing that every visitor you sent to that room would face the temptation of staying with him in an apparition. It's too easy to lose yourself to dreaming when reality feels like nothing but sorrow."

"And all these years, I never realized he was there. It's a wonder I could help anyone."

Katterina reached over and took the woman's hands in hers for a moment. "You helped so many to see they must make the choice and live the lives they had been given. To quit wishing for what could never be. I know I had to. Perhaps that is why God allowed him to stay for so long."

Dorothea squeezed Katterina's hand in gratitude. "Oh, thank you, my dear. I needed to hear that. It's too easy to question if it was all worth it when we near the end."

Katterina sat back, withdrawing her hands as she struggled to swallow. She quickly flicked away a tear. "So Dietz was the one who was able to get rid of Nicolas? I must thank him in the morning."

"Aye, the God of heaven has a plan for that one, though there is a darkness that still struggles to win him back." She rocked for another moment, distracted, and then shook her head. "Ah, but where was I?"

"Ysentrude was freed?"

"Yes, after Dietz sent Nicolas far away. It wasn't long after that Ysentrude wanted to be freed. I've been fading ever since. The God of heaven is almost done with me here."

"But the young man—"

"You must talk to your prince—Dietz needs to go with you. He mustn't stay on to take care of an old woman."

"We can't just leave you here to fade away"—she couldn't say *die*—"on your own."

The front door broke open, a cold gust of night air blasting in. An unholy screech ripped through the dim light as half-a-dozen booted feet stomped into the home. "You're through, old woman!"

A shock of lightning shot from an outstretched pointing finger of a caped intruder toward Dorothea. Katterina jumped up, ready to throw herself in the way of the bolt, but a burly man grabbed her, choking her from behind. She hissed, scratching and clawing at her assailant, but he wouldn't release her. She could feel the rough wool of his black cape as he began to squeeze the air from her. A grunt escaped her throat, and just as her vision was dimming she saw Jacob dash into the room, staff in hand.

The warrior monk shouted a prayer and the lightning dissipated. The other two intruders rushed Jacob, but he used his staff to drive them backward. Paul burst in and stood by his mentor's side, slashing with his sword, and several knights followed. Katterina tried to use the commotion to her advantage, elbowing the man behind her, but his grip only tightened. Jacob leapt over the body of another intruder. He whipped his staff around his head and brought it down on the head of her assailant. The man gave a jerk and his grip lessened, giving Katterina a chance to bound away. Jacob cracked the man in the chest with his staff and the man crumpled to the ground. The monk was on top of him at once, ready to bind his hands and feet with leather strips, but there was no need. The collapsed assailant gasped and clutched at his chest, writhing, unable to cause further damage. At last, his breathing ceased. The two other intruders were bleeding out, unseeing eyes staring at the rafters above. It was over just as Amis and the last of the knights ran in.

Katterina turned to see Dietz kneeling next to the burned form of Dorothea. The acrid aroma of cooked flesh mixed with the metallic smell of pooling blood. She sputtered for air, wanting to flee. The young man keened, his grief rending the air, followed shortly by Helena's wail as Rapunzel walked into the room with the babe on her hip.

"What happened?" Katterina's daughter asked, green eyes wide, her uncovered hair stuck up in its curly mess.

"They came for me!" the young man sobbed. "I should never have run away, never put Dorothea in danger. If only I had done as I was told, she'd still be alive!"

"Who came for you? Who are these—?" Jacob pointed with his staff to the men lying dead on the floor. Katterina could see the whorl tattoo matching Dietz's on each of their jawlines, visible only because they remained clean-shaven. But they were light-skinned and fair-haired, like most Allerians.

"This is my family—part of the coven that raised me."

"The ones left behind?"

"Yes, to guard the Wood and prepare for war."

"But why would they come—"

"They came for me, I should never have—"

"Yes, yes, you should never have come here, you said so

before!" Katterina snapped. But Dietz was hurting, afraid. Such a speech would not make things better. "Listen, we need to understand why they came for you. And why were they angry at Dorothea? Why kill—" She had to stop, breathe. Katterina's eyes found Rapunzel's. Her daughter was weeping silently, swaying to calm Helena, who had tangled her hands in Rapunzel's short curls.

Paul knelt beside the young man. "Listen, Dietz, we can't understand you. You said that the coven had left to seek further orders from someone in the Eastern Ports and left only a remnant behind to prepare for war."

"To hold the power here."

Paul shook his head. "I don't know what that means."

"The coven maintains the darkness here. They knew that someone in this wood was fighting the darkness with light, but they didn't know who. We each went out to find the keeper of the light, to destroy him or her. But they knew when they regrouped that I was not among them. I hoped they would give up and leave me alone. Dorothea is secluded, her home protected by the God of heaven. How could they have tracked me here?"

"Or they were tracking us. I sensed something in the Wood before we arrived here." Rapunzel hiccuped, a pitiful sound Katterina knew her daughter hated.

Paul shook his head and shot a glance at Jacob. "No, we would have known—wouldn't we?"

Jacob only shook his head. "I knew something was wrong, but there were no tracks. Still, I should have known better than to drop my guard."

Everyone grew silent, but Katterina looked at Amis. He seemed unsurprised.

THE THREAT

*E*dmund was used to the memories coming against him from time to time, but why wouldn't they leave him alone and let him sleep? As he stood at the bow of the ship looking over into the waves, it felt as though they were crashing into him, threatening to pull him under. He lifted his eyes to the horizon, and slowly, everything around him—the ship, the moonlight, old Hazm on watch—faded from his vision. The waters sparkled, suddenly reflecting memories, like a portal into Edmund's past.

There he stood: a small, defenseless boy. The baker towered over him, his harsh voice cracking in frustration. The boy's face twisted in agony, resolute, refusing to give ground. No, he wouldn't make the wishes anymore. But the baker was determined to get what he wanted. The man's voice lashed out, as did his whip, and when little Edmund still refused, the man threatened his own wife, Cibell. Little Edmund's knees buckled. She was the only kind person in Edmund's life. He would do as the baker wanted.

A sea monster broke through the waves on the starboard side, crashing through his memory-vision and coming face-to-face with him. It was long and sleek, black scales covering its snake-like form, with purple gills opening on the sides of its neck. The pale silver eyes had vertical reptilian slits that rounded slightly as they centered on Edmund. Its maw opened, revealing gruesome fangs and a forked tongue. "Little man, what are you doing?"

Edmund tried to breathe. Though he had never seen her in her monstrous shape, he knew that voice. He looked around the deck, noticing that Hazm was frozen in place. How did Camilla have that kind of power?

"I'm—I'm—" What was he doing? He didn't know how to respond.

One tentacle slid up from beneath the waters and tapped the side of the ship, like an impatient woman tapping her foot. "You're quite busy, trying to learn to rule a kingdom, aren't you?"

"It's what I'm supposed to do."

"Why?"

"It's the life I was meant for."

"Before you were stolen."

"Yes."

"And that's why you are dancing around on deck, playing with swords?"

It was odd to see something as gargantuan as this monster tilt her massive head and blink her eyes as though thoughtfully considering everything with great care.

"Things could be easier. Much easier," she breathed.

Edmund swallowed. He wanted to look away, to retreat to his bunk, but he couldn't.

"Just make a wissshhhh." Her rough voice hissed the last syllable, and then the tentacle and her monstrous head slipped back beneath the waves. Edmund blinked and reached for the side of the bow to steady himself. He jerked back when he realized it was still wet from where she had touched. What had just happened?

He looked around. That's when he saw Gwynndolen, her pale-white skin nearly the color of her chemise, her bright braid muted by the moonlight. Her dark eyes were enormous, her mouth slack with surprise.

"What—?" she said.

Edmund crossed the deck to her, grateful to see that Hazm had roused and was looking over at them in confusion.

"Your Highness! You shouldn't let her be on deck at night. Could you take her below?"

"Exactly what I was planning on doing." He put his arm around the maid, and she didn't resist as he turned her toward the narrow stairs.

"But *what was that?*" Gwynndolen spoke in an awed whisper as she climbed down carefully.

"What was what?"

"That—that *thing!* It was huge, and threatening you. Or telling you to do something. Or—or—" Her voice was getting louder, as though she might grow hysterical. She spun around to face him in the narrow corridor.

Edmund cleared his throat as he looked down at her. "What are you talking about? I saw you go on deck and I wanted to make sure you were safe."

Gwynndolen frowned, her face puckering in confusion. "But I saw—"

"You saw what? I think you've been walking in your sleep. Here's your cabin. You'd best—"

She grabbed his arm. "Edmund." Her voice revealed she was no longer sleepy, no longer dazed. She knew her mind and would not be dissuaded by a smooth lie. "What. Was. That. Thing?"

"Don't worry about it." He tried to smile, and failed. "It's only a nightmare. My nightmare. Nothing to do with you."

"Edmund—"

He didn't know what she wanted to say, but she couldn't help him. Nothing she could say or do could free him from the darkness he was bound to. "Go to bed, Lady Gwynndolen." He reached around her and opened the door. She stumbled backward, but he caught her, turned her around, and gave her a gentle push forward. "Good night." He shut the door behind her, wishing he could shut the door on his own nightmare with such ease.

DARKNESS

$\mathcal{U}$nable to sleep since she learned of Ute's death, Amee had found solace in sitting alone. Was she falling apart again, like she had when their mother had died, and then again after she was separated from her sisters? How could she be expected to make plans and delegate tasks to make certain spies were in key places for the upcoming war? She couldn't sleep, she couldn't eat. At times, she couldn't even shift into her centaur form. She simply sat on the floor, unbathed, dark hair wild, clothing rumpled.

Nofra came to her each morning and each evening, trying to get her to take food, sometimes convincing her to drink. Amee pushed the thought of the young woman away. She could not hold close the maid who called her "mother." Not when she would need to betray her.

While her body sat motionless, she reached out with her spirit, yearning for some hint that Camilla would break through the barrier that kept them apart. She needed her sister, the one with strength, with her impulsive ability to make decisions—even wrong decisions—and plunge ahead.

Amee was stuck, Ute's plans falling apart now that there was nothing to keep her on track.

And then it hit. Another shock wave rolled through her being, jolting her as it had when Ute had called the sisters to her castle deep within the Soontrisse Mountains. Her black eyes looked beyond the cramped room she was sitting in; what was she seeing? What was before her?

Deep down in the darkness, her eyes followed a path, almost a tunnel, but not one a human or even an animal would make. No, it was wild, untamed. More gnarled paths flowed together beneath the ground, reaching out, interweaving with so many others—but what were they?

She tried to even her intake of breath, to slow down her heart as she held each breath a little longer. Her focus became clearer. She was traveling along the roots of . . . something. Large roots, deep beneath the ground. Darkness was spreading, not just from being beneath the ground, but a spiritual darkness was permeating the land.

Death.

A light of some sort had gone out . . .

The woman in the Dark Wood—she had died! At last!

Beneath the ground, the darkness now could feed into the trees along the way, connecting the Eastern Ports all the way to and throughout the Dark Wood, with no other force to resist. And if all this on the land was finally connecting, then her followers would more easily find their way here, at last, to complete the quest and bring the war again.

But he would stay there, safe. The darkness would shield him, and he would remain. She could do anything so long as he was safe.

Amee felt an unexpected pang reach deep within her. Was it worth it? Another life lost so they could attain power? She shook her head, her tangled hair whipping around her face. *No!* She wouldn't think such things. If it wasn't worth it, then Ute had died in vain and her complete life had lacked purpose. All these years cut off, even the years spent in service to her father before he sacrificed their mother—it would all be pointless. It couldn't be. She clenched her fists, uncaring of the sharp pain when her jagged nails cut into her palms. She wouldn't let the sacrifices they had made be for nothing.

⁂

RAPUNZEL HELD Helena close to her heart. The child whimpered as they stood beneath the thick canopy of leaves next to the hollow grave. Slowly Paul and Jacob eased Dorothea's blanket-wrapped body into the ground. Rapunzel shuddered when Dietz keened again. "I don't know what I'll do," the young man moaned, glancing back over his shoulder. There, behind them, the intruders who had been his family lay in freshly dug graves.

Rapunzel couldn't stop shivering as she thought of them, now interred deep inside the earth, soon to decay, becoming food for the darkness of the trees. Trees she had always loved and felt at home among now seemed twisted, crooked, reaching into her nightmares and calling forth her terror. Paul had made the decision that they needed to bury the bodies. They could not light a pyre without setting the Wood aflame. *But perhaps it needs to burn,* Rapunzel's mind murmured as the oppressive shadows pressed down.

Jacob's voice lifted, defying the darkness, and he called on the God she had so recently entrusted her life to. She moved Helena, settling the babe on her other hip. Could the God who met her beneath the mountains also meet her here in the Dark Wood? She knew with her mind that he could, but found she needed to listen intently to Jacob's words to believe there would be comfort. The warrior monk was speaking of Jesu the Christ—how he spent his last night on the earth before he was crucified. His deep voice dipped as he told of how Christ knew of the betrayal, how he was unsurprised. Dietz continued to cry, but quieted when the monk placed a dark hand on his shoulder. "Christ did not berate his companions, but he spent the night teaching one last time, knowing they would recall it later, when they could better understand. He, who was to face the ultimate torture, spoke of peace."

Jacob's voice faded away as Rapunzel became aware of the holy presence of God. There were no words, just a rush of comfort and peace shoring up her weak areas, as though she was being cradled and rocked gently, just as she was holding Helena. Tears soaked her face. Conflict rose. *In my heart*, she admitted to her Savior, *I feel betrayed*. Not only by losing Dorothea, but in what was coming. How could God expect her to give Helena up? And to a family that had offered the child to a witch as their amends! Her uncertainties and fears went beyond that, though. She was afraid for the moments that led beyond the Dark Wood, the paths that would carry them to the Eastern Ports. Could she become queen while missing the child she had grown to love? Would she embarrass her husband and kingdom among a group of people raised as nobles?

Peace descended again, and shafts of light breaking through the branches above pierced the darkness of the Wood. God had not set her on this path to abandon her. He had paid the ultimate price for her life. It did not mean she was always safe on this earth, but it did mean God always cared for her.

Once more, she noticed Jacob's voice and the surrounding people. The monk had turned the young man to look at him and had him by the shoulders. "Jesu said, 'Peace

I leave with you, my peace I give to you. And I do not give as the world gives, only to take it away . . .'"

Rapunzel felt her mother's hand on her own shoulder, and she reached to grasp it. How many years had Katterina known Dorothea? How hard was this awkward trip for her? She caught a glint of humor in her mother's eyes, though tears also clouded them. Yes, her mother's sorrow was mixed with mirth. The woman was likely remembering some silly moment with Dorothea, when Katterina had still been Cat. Rapunzel let her tears continue to fall as she kissed the top of Helena's knit cap. She prayed Dietz would find the peace she was now experiencing in the darkness's midst.

AN INVITATION

Gwynndolen was grateful to have solid ground beneath her feet, and she thanked God silently for the clear sky so that she could exercise the horses. They would hate getting back on board, but even this small respite was good for them. She and her brothers spent the morning riding and riding, making certain each horse got the exercise it needed before they were each allowed time in a pasture near the docks. It was late morning when she saw the prince approaching.

"Edmund needs cheering," Georgius said, looking her way.

"Why tell me?"

He shrugged. "No reason at all."

"If anything, I only upset him more . . ." Her voice dipped low as she thought of the nightmare he wouldn't explain to her. "He can't stand to be around me."

Georgius nodded. "Oh, so *that's* why he's always watching you and looking for a reason to come and speak with you."

"He doesn't." She looked around, grateful her older brother wasn't speaking in the hearing of Liam or Beatrix.

Georgius let out a laugh and patted her shoulder before marching over toward the prince, who was heading their way. The men met each other halfway and instantly began talking. Georgius now laughed full-out at something the prince said and thumped him on the back before turning back to his sister. "Gwynndolen, Edmund has heard there is to be an island festival tonight. You've never been to one of those, right?"

"No, I don't know what that is." She looked at Edmund, her interest piqued, but Georgius continued.

"I've only been to one myself. If I remember right, there will be games and dancing. At the Eastern Ports I've heard they sometimes set off lights that color the sky and give off loud booms, but they won't have that tonight."

"Loud booms? I'm glad we won't have that!"

Edmund looked confused. "Whyever not? The lightning colors are wondrous to behold."

"I'm sure they are, for people, but the horses—"

"Don't you ever think of anything besides your horses?"

"They aren't *my* horses, they are the High King's tribute and I've been entrusted—"

"Yes, yes, I know, you must take care of them for your father's sake and all that."

"I would think you would appreciate that in your servants, Your Highness."

Edmund's lips twisted in a held-back smile. "Georgius, make Liam watch the horses tonight. I admire Lady Gwynndolen's dedication to her charges, but tonight she shall be free to join us and have what some of us call 'fun.'"

Gwynndolen felt her mouth drop open.

"Careful," the prince taunted, no longer stopping his smile, "you'll catch flies that way." And with that he winked at her and walked toward the carriage that was pulling up to collect his family.

"But—" she sputtered, too late.

"You'll have fun, and there will be no loud booms to upset the horses. We don't have to board them till early in the morning, and Liam will take good care of them here." Georgius indicated the stables she had already inspected. The feed here was good, and she knew he was right. The horses would be fine, but would she?

A TALE OF THREE BROTHERS

*A*mis noticed how Dietz sat slumped before the fire on a resting day after they left Dorothea's cottage. The young man looked as though his family came from the Eastern Ports, but he spoke perfect Allerian. All on the trip accommodated his presence by speaking Allerian, except for the knights who had never been taught anything but the Northland language.

As was the custom of knights, they all gathered around their own fire nearby, taking turns keeping watch. Jacob walked between the two groups, making certain his men were alert. Paul was playing with little Helena, who kept trying to stuff leaves in her mouth. Rapunzel walked around, stretching her slender body after being hunched over, tending to the child inside the cramped carriage. Poor princess—if only she had not been so stubborn and had brought Jehanne along to help care for the squirming toddler. Katterina was walking with her daughter, and the two women spoke in hushed tones. Amis could see in their reddened eyes how disturbed they were. Dorothea's death hung over them like an oppressive shadow, while the knowledge of returning Helena to her home continued to weigh on them.

All these thoughts swirled in Amis's mind as he finished stirring the stew over the fire. Serving it into wooden bowls, he whispered a prayer. If only he could lighten the darkness that pushed upon these people. But the truth was heavy, and the only way out was *through*.

Amis began making his rounds, serving the modest fare he had prepared. He served the nobles first, then the knights, with himself and Dietz last. The young man fiddled with his spoon in the thickened broth.

"I'm sure it's not nearly as good as what Dorothea made for you."

Dietz perked up. "*With* me. I was not a poor cook when I first came to her. With her help, I became quite good."

"Is that so?" Paul asked, now seated before the fire with Helena on his lap. He reached for his stew. "Well, we will need to have you aid our humble Amis while on this trip."

Amis appreciated Paul's quick thinking. He knew from his own experience that serving others gave him space to process disappointments. Dietz would need that. Stories helped, too. He noticed Rapunzel staring at him with expectation bright in her emerald eyes, and he took his last bite of stew and set the bowl down. "Dishes will have to wait, I've a story to tell in this Dark Wood."

Rapunzel smiled. "I was hoping so."

Amis wished it were a happier tale, but it had to be told. Maybe tomorrow he could make them laugh. "You know, there was once a family of brothers, and each one of them wanted to grow up very rich, though for different reasons. The eldest thought it the most important thing a man could attain in life. The middle thought it the best way to provide for a family. And the youngest thought it would help him achieve freedom.

"Their father was a poor serf who had no land of his own in the rice paddies of the Eastern Ports. His skin was as dark as yours, Jacob, as he worked beneath the scorching sun where the mosquitos swarmed. A good, hard-working man, he wanted better for his sons. He and his wife agreed they would not see their boys indentured to the cruel lord whose land they worked. When each son came of age, they would hide the young man and teach him to run away by night, making him promise never to return. Their father was unselfish, willing to set them free.

"The eldest ran away in a hurry and never even glanced behind after a quick goodbye. On the first night, he found himself an inn where he could sleep, and he used a few coins to buy food to last a week. Unused to such rest, he slept in each morning and spent his time in the tavern, drinking and gambling away what little he had left, hoping to gain more money by luck. Instead, his gambling indentured him, and he sold himself to the innkeeper to pay off his debts. His days became early mornings and late nights filled with cleaning rooms, washing dishes, and caring for the horses of guests who visited.

"Two years passed, and though the eldest never sent a word of how he was or what he was doing, his family tried not to worry. Perhaps he was well, living a good life somewhere far off. It came time for the middle son to run away, and he did, but he glanced over his shoulder, wishing he could take his family with him. When he arrived late that night at the inn where his indentured brother worked, he greeted him gladly but did not stay. He ate a modest meal and then slept in the Wood nearby, saving his coins. He rose early in the morning as he had always done and began looking for work immediately. He liked living near his brother, and was delighted when, on his second inquiry, he discovered a blacksmith willing to take on an apprentice. He worked hard as his father had taught him to do and soon became a valued member of the blacksmith's family. This in no way replaced the family of his youth. He often thought of them fondly. The young man knew he could never go back, and so began a family of his own. The blacksmith's daughter was a handsome girl, and a year and a day after they wed, she gave him a little girl. All seemed well until the youngest brother found him."

Amis took a sip of tea and looked at his companions. Dietz kept shifting while the others sat entranced. The tale was having its way.

"Now the third son was the youngest by far, and it had been many years since his older brothers had left. Life had grown worse for their father, as the lord of the land had died and his malicious son had taken the title. This new lord demanded a greater portion of the crops with each passing year, and ordered more animals brought for his table. The demands left little for even their shrinking family to live on. During this time, the mother became ill, and there was no money to help her get well. She passed away, leaving a silence the two men found unbearable.

"The father knew the malicious lord was cunning and had seen that his other sons had escaped servitude. As soon as he felt the boy was able, he sent the youngest away, even though he wasn't of age yet. The boy got away, escaping by passing stolen scraps of meat to the snapping hounds that were chasing him as he ran faster than he had thought possible. The father cried, but not tears of sorrow for himself and his lonely state. He was awash with relief that he had done as he and his wife had set out to do. His sons were free to live a better life than before. At night he knelt in his cold, empty home and sang quiet songs of praise to the God of heaven.

"But the youngest son hated leaving his father behind with no sons to help him harvest the rice or care for the animals. He knew the malicious young lord would increase his taxes and make the old man's life a greater misery. When the youngest son came to the town where his brothers had settled, he enlisted their help. He was determined they would set their father free.

"'But how can we go back?' whined the eldest. 'I'm indentured here.'

"'I would like to return, but the lord would then have me in his grasp, and who would provide for my wife and child?' mourned the middle.

"'Would you really leave your father to languish and die alone in his old age?' the youngest sputtered.

"The two could not meet his eyes. They stared at the floor as though the dirt might suddenly become a lush carpet.

"'We can do this, we *must* do this for the man who loved us so well. I have a plan, and our cause is just.'

"And so he told them what they would do.

"First, the youngest brother took what his father had saved for him and paid off the price of his oldest brother's servitude. The middle brother kissed his wife and child good-bye, promising to return. Creeping back to their childhood home by the dark of a moonless night, they found their father in his bed, all alone.

"'Come with us,' whispered the youngest.

"'Yes, you shall all come live with me.' The middle smiled as he spoke the words, though no one could see him. 'Though my quarters are tight, my wife bade me to bring you to our hearth.'

"The old father sat upright in shock, as though a night-mare had woke him. 'But you should not have come back!' he cried, his voice dry and rusty as though he had not spoken in the week since the youngest had left. 'The malicious lord has been watching for you.'

"The youngest son gave a giggle, not a manly sound at all. 'Just let him try to capture us!'

"For as they ran, the old father surprisingly spry, the youngest deterred the hounds that chased after. Their growls turned to happy yelps of gratitude as he once more tossed them meat. The knights were gaining ground, but at the marsh their horses halted, rearing back and tossing their heads at the sudden bright light that flashed off the water ahead, making the night as bright as day.

"There, on the edge of the waters, was the sorceress Amee, pawing the ground in her centaur form. The youngest son, meaning well, had pledged himself to her by spilling some of his blood at the edge of the marsh. She had agreed to help him lose the knights, giving him a week's time to free his father and lead the malicious lord's soldiers to the marsh.

"Now, the soldiers' horses bucked at the site of the centaur woman, and the men fell, one of them stomped to death as the horses scattered. Amee charged the other three, making quick work of slicing them up with an enormous sword no mortal could lift. Her black eyes grew even larger as she became human once more and piled up the bodies, then chose one to eat, impervious to the audience behind her.

"The father and older brothers twisted away from the sorceress as she tore into the flesh, smacking noisily.

"'What have you done?' the old man cried out.

"'I freed you,' the youngest said with a smile and shrug.

"'But at what cost?'

"'He's mine now.' Amee's voice was husky as she wiped her mouth with a blood-soaked hand. 'He'll do as I say.'

"Though she allowed the family to leave her, enveloping herself in a cloud of darkness as they left, when they tried to begin new lives in the village, they noted the changes in the youngest brother. Amee called to him, and his eyes grew darker than the eyes of a Ronan. Each time she asked him to do something, her power grew. The dark magic wove its spell over him, and it was not long before he retreated to the marsh and kept himself with her alone. He was hers and did as she bid.

"To save his family, he lost himself." Amis patted Dietz's shoulder. "You think to sacrifice one thing, but she takes so much more."

The young man's eyes grew wide. "How did you know my father's story? Even Dorothea didn't know—not all of it."

"She knew enough and loved you," Amis said.

Jacob had sat for the story and now tapped a finger to his broad lips before speaking. "Your father was the youngest in this story?"

"Yes. He served Amee the rest of his life. They told me he died not long after my brother died. But—" His shoulders rounded and his head ducked. "I was so young when I was sent away from the Eastern Ports. I don't remember them. I don't remember *her*."

"So you, like me, are from the Eastern Ports?"

"I wish I were—I mean, my family, the one I was born to, is from the Eastern Ports. But I'm not like you. A monk. Made to serve God. I was born to serve the coven. To serve *her* purpose. They sent me away from the marsh to the Dark Wood's coven. Said there was a reason, wouldn't say why."

"How did they ever let you go off by yourself?"

Dietz shrugged, but Amis could tell that didn't satisfy Jacob. The fool clapped his hands to lighten the mood. "All will be revealed in time, dear monk! We have much ahead of us yet."

Paul dodged his spoon out of Helena's grasping fingers. "Not sure I like the sound of that. Our Amis is a prophetic fool. He knows and gathers our stories—"

"And I use them for good!" Amis stood and began collecting the dishes.

Dietz slumped. "What good could come from my family's horror?"

Amis looked over at Jacob, who nodded thoughtfully before commenting. "Your story is not fully written, so we can't yet tell. But the shape of it . . . it holds promise. I think the God of heaven isn't done with you yet. Now that you travel with us, we will see what is to come."

THE COST OF RULING

Before Edmund helped the queen into the carriage, he gave one more glance back at Gwynndolen. He noticed how the sun glinted off her red curls in much the same way as it sparkled on the waters. Time for such thoughts disappeared as the carriage jerked away once he was seated.

When they arrived at the small island's castle, King Tasufin welcomed the trio to a banquet table laden with food and gave them an earful of his own praises. The island's tribute to the High King this summer would be leaving in a week's time, and would hopefully not be plundered by the pirates who routinely traveled in the Illyan Sea.

King Tasufin was a small man with swarthy features. He spoke with the accent of the Eastern Ports but without the decorum and reverence common to those people. This man, Edmund quickly deduced, cared only for money and position. King Purnell did as he always did with other rulers, giving a thin smile and listening, indicating neither pleasure nor displeasure. The island wasn't exactly on their way to the

High King's court, but his father must have had his reasons for stopping here first.

"Yes," King Tasufin was saying, stroking his crooked little beard, "the High King depends on our shipments of dried fruit, and also this bean he likes us to roast for him, called 'coffy.' Most people don't know, but he struggles with his health. This brew"—he gestured to the dark, bitter liquid that served to balance the sweetness of the dessert—"has become a favorite of the High King. He uses it to manage his morning, umm, headaches."

Edmund's father gave a rare nod of approval. "I see you have increased your usefulness to His Majesty."

"That is what we do, isn't it? We find what will make our land and our people invaluable and thereby increase our worth. We have watched you do it for years, and we have learned by watching."

King Purnell lifted his mug of coffy to his host before sipping. "To our continued success in courting the favor of the High King. May His Majesty never find a reason to be displeased with his servants."

King Tasufin lifted his own mug. "And to the advantageous alliances such servants can make with one another." But he didn't drink right away, his smile changing the shape of his moustache as his gaze turned to include Edmund and his daughter, Subh. "We have not told you that our daughter will be accompanying us this year. To these two young people who are at last joining us at court," he said, as he raised his mug still higher.

Edmund shifted in his seat, barely able to choke down his drink. He stared at the bright tapestry across from him, not daring a glance at the lovely, dark princess whose delicate facial features must take after her deceased mother.

"We did not know that Princess Subh was of age already."

"Indeed, only just this spring. We hope to have her betrothed before court is dismissed." He stared openly at Edmund.

Queen Lefwenna raised her glass, having taken only one sip of the coffy and quickly exchanged it for wine. "To her betrothal, then. May it be someone near you, so that you will get to see your grandchildren grow and comfort you in your old age."

Though the kings drank to the queen's toast, neither seemed happy as the conversation shifted.

Back in the carriage, Edmund's father spoke his mind. "My dear, we know that you have the best intentions for our son, but if he is to take the throne, there are some things that must be calculated. His betrothal must be something that will make the kingdom stronger, and those at court who would take advantage of his naivete—"

"My what?"

The king turned to Edmund with a frown on his face. "We have done our best to instruct you, and you have done well to learn as much as you have, but that does not mean that you will hold your own at court this summer."

"What have I done to displease Your Majesty?"

"It is not your fault—you have not been raised to this life, and there is the question of your—" But the king faltered here, looking to the queen for help.

"Edmund," she began with a dry voice. She cleared her throat and tried again. "The business with Rapunzel, and then this past winter, the thing you won't let us speak about. You promised to never wish again, but—"

"Such a promise is ludicrous when one is the king. Your mother disagrees with our royal person on this point. She has stated emphatically that you must never wish again, but it's not that simple. If it is necessary to keep the kingdom together, we ourself believe that God has granted you such a gift and such a position to do well by our kingdom's people."

"You mean, you think *God* wants me to use this wish? Has my mother not explained the cost?"

The king shook his head. "You are speaking of Camilla, the sorceress confined to the sea? She is the High King's problem. The sisters of sorcery focused their troubles over there—my father only sent troops to aid them because he was allied to King Matar, the old High King. Had he known what the war would do to our people and how it would subjugate us to a new High King, our people might never have been sent to fight.

"Your mother says you must never wish, but we say that you must do whatever is necessary to be a good king. She is a good queen, and a good mother, but she is more of a mother than a queen, and you are not a little boy. Nor are you a troubadour any longer, dancing about with a lute to entertain in someone else's Great Hall. You can handle your gift. You did so after the incident this winter, and you will again, if and when the time comes."

The queen wanted to say something, but the king caught her hands in his own. "My dear," he said, quieting her. "Now, Edmund, hear me. You have enough disadvantages that you must use what you do have to become the leader our people need. You have nothing but opportunities before you. We are not a young king, and you are not a young man. No, we are not saying to wish left and right, but if a king offers his daughter's hand and something stands in the way of the happiness of your people—wish it away. Care for your people!"

"I cannot use the wish and not expect consequences!"

"Then we will deal with them together. God has allowed you this gift, and he will provide a way for you to use it. That is why you have been chosen to be our heir."

"I thought I was your heir regardless."

"Why not use what you have? You must marry well, you must make advantageous alliances—you must use *everything* at your disposal! Each opportunity must be evaluated for its useful properties to the kingdom, and that alone should rule your decisions as heir to the throne. No more being caught up in the moment, no more dancing away from your responsibilities."

Edmund couldn't speak; he didn't know what to say. What could he say in the light of his father's utilitarian logic?

THE SUMMER OF THE TWIN LADIES

By midafternoon, Gwynndolen had made her way back aboard only to find that Beatrix was already in their cramped cabin getting ready for the evening. Her sister wrinkled her nose at once. She clenched her hands into tight balls and began looking through her things for something suitable to wear for the evening. "Gwynndolen, why—"

"Enough!" Gwynndolen spun to face her. She could feel her face contorting with fury, and she took a steadying breath at the look Beatrix was now giving her, as though she expected a blow. Had she ever hit her sister? Oh yes—once she had, but that had been long ago. In the span of a moment, memories washed over her.

The summer of the twin ladies. Gwynndolen recalled their visit when they came from across the Illyan Sea. She had been twelve, maybe younger—sometime after their father had grown ill. The visitors were nasty, waspish ladies who liked to sit around and needle everyone with insults as they exchanged gossip. Their hands were always busy with embroidery, and their tongues were never at rest. The only solace Gwynndolen found that stifling summer was when her mother extended mercy and allowed her to begin training horses. Georgius and Liam were in training alongside the knights. Gwynndolen was given more and more leeway as the summer progressed, easing the burden of her brothers and decreasing her time spent with other womenfolk. It made sense to everyone that, since she was born to the stablemaster before being orphaned, she would be good with horses. Of course she should excel at training and caring for them.

Had she felt a bit guilty leaving her mother and Beatrix to entertain the ladies? Yes, but Beatrix had seemed to enjoy it. Staring into Beatrix's dark eyes, she could almost feel the heat of shame flush her skin again as another memory rattled around in her head. The twin ladies had come out to the stables one afternoon and found her hard at work, sweating like a man. And Beatrix, beside them, ridiculed her. "She was born common, you know. She'll never do well at court!" her sister had spouted—the first time Beatrix had ever humiliated her for her birth.

Things had never been the same after that summer.

Now, back once again in their shared cabin, her anger bloomed into one concise question. "Why do you despise me so?"

"Despise you?"

"Yes—nothing I ever do seems good enough, but there was a time when we got along. You didn't care that I was born to the stablemaster and his wife. Do you remember? We were great friends when we were young, before you decided you hated me. And you act as though it's more than just me. It's as though you hate our home."

"I don't hate our home."

Gwynndolen stripped down to her chemise and began the task of scrubbing away the smell of hard work. She could have Dyanys, their maid, wait on her, but why? She could do this for herself. "Something in you does. You have always tried to get invited to the halls of other lords and ladies. You compared everything we did with how others lived and what we needed to change. I was nothing short of embarrassing to you! Why? Why did we no longer get along after the twin ladies came from Alleria?"

"How could we get along, Gwynndolen? You abandoned me. You turned up your nose at everything I liked. You were out in the heat and the muck helping train the horses. I couldn't do that, could I now?"

An image of Beatrix standing nearby, looking forlorn, caught in her memory like a burr that she needed to tease out of her horse's mane. But Beatrix had been the one who had mocked Gwynndolen's love of training. Her sister had been the one to start it, hadn't she? "You were always with the—"

"Even before they came, and especially after they came, you found as many excuses as possible to get out of lessons, to abandon your needlework."

"Father was ill. Any of us who were good with the horses were needed to—"

"And those of us who weren't good with the horses had no use at all."

"What?"

"Nothing."

Was that a tear on her sister's lashes? She took a tentative step forward. "Beatrix, what do you mean? You never liked the horses—"

"No, Gwynndolen, the horses never liked me. I wanted to be good with them, like you, like the others, but I—" She swallowed and then turned away. But really, where could she go? The quarters were quite tight.

"I always thought that—well, that you hated the horses."

"You spent all that time last summer teaching Lady

Rapunzel how to not be afraid of the horses and how to ride, but did it ever occur to you or Georgius or any of the others that I wanted that same help?" Beatrix had picked up a brush, but wasn't brushing her hair.

"But you know how to ride."

"When? How long since you have seen me ride?"

Gwynndolen thought for quite a while. Of course she had long known that her sister didn't have an affinity for Gwynndolen's beloved horses. But Beatrix had always acted as though it was because she hated them and preferred the comfort of the carriage. She preened and acted as though she enjoyed her needlework and gossip more than spending time outdoors doing what her family was best at.

"Sometimes it feels as though mother and father knew what a disappointment I would be and were perfectly happy to adopt a daughter who could handle horses."

Gwynndolen reached for Beatrix and turned her back around. "They couldn't have known when we were so young who would be good with what."

Beatrix just shook her head.

"And all this time, I just thought that *you* thought I was unacceptable."

Beatrix held her arms around herself. "It doesn't really matter now, does it? You enjoy your horses and leave the rest to me. Soon it won't matter, I'll find my way at court this summer and you'll just—"

"I could teach you."

Beatrix let her facade slip enough for Gwynndolen to see how hurt she really was. "I don't think I have the knack for learning that."

"I think we all possess the ability to learn more than we thought possible, Beatrix. If you truly want to do well at court, you'll also have to ride. I can't believe I didn't—" She let her words fall silent as she saw her sister, perhaps for the first time. "But it's something I can help you with, if you'll let me."

Beatrix gave a quick nod, and then recovered her composure. "Only if you allow me to help you. I can't let you attend the festival like that!"

"What do you mean?"

"I mean, I'll get Dyanys and we'll soon have you smelling fresh and looking beautiful. Pretty enough to tempt a prince!" She giggled. "Don't worry, sister, I mean you no ill will. You help me with what you're best at, and I'll help you, too."

Gwynndolen wasn't sure how she felt about that.

OF LOSS AND GAIN

apunzel could barely breathe when the cottage came into view. It looked just as she remembered it. She had hoped in her heart of hearts that there would not be anyone here. After all, it had not been Helga's cottage the last time Rapunzel had worked here. The brothers and their wives had merely gathered in their late mother's cottage to discern what to do about the witch's curse.

Rapunzel noted the fresh green plants poking up in the fields as they approached that spoke of a working farm. As their party drew near a small cottage, a woman came into view, kneeling on the soil, obviously tending the family garden. Rapunzel said nothing to Katterina; she simply handed her Helena and left the carriage. Paul and Jacob were already off their horses, Paul helping Rapunzel out. They took slow steps as they approached the bewildered gardener, who looked startled at the group coming onto her land.

"My lord?" Rapunzel could hear the woman as she saw her wipe dirty hands on her apron and give an awkward bow of her head.

"We are looking for someone."

The woman stayed on her knees as though too tired to stand.

"My husband is out in the fields and—" She gave a double glance at Rapunzel. "You—I know you! You served me well during a hard time." This was the Helga Rapunzel remembered. The woman still had those bright blue eyes, rosy-red apple cheeks, and a large smile.

Rapunzel nodded and gestured to Paul who approached and gave Helga a smile. "Helga, meet my husband, Prince Paul of the Fisher King's realm."

"A prince?" she gasped. "Oh, my, if I had known you were coming—!" She seemed unwieldy, her balance unsteady as she launched herself up on her feet and then gave a lopsided curtsy. True, she seemed rounder than Rapunzel recalled, but—

"Helga! Are you with child?"

The woman gave a booming laugh, full of joy. "I am! Our family was released from the terrible curse we were under."

"I am happy for you," she forced, but even as she said the words she saw Helga's face fall. Rapunzel tried again to smile, knowing her voice had betrayed her distress. How could she congratulate Helga, knowing what it had cost little Helena?

"No, you aren't. You didn't approve of what we decided to do. But it was the only way to free us from the witch's curse. And she only took one baby." Her lovely, rosy face had drooped, cheeks becoming wet with tears. "Ah, me! I cry so easily now. Two babes in two years' time . . . ."

"It *was* your child the witch took?"

"Yes, a little girl. I saw her for only a moment, but her life bought us freedom."

Something ugly twisted inside Rapunzel. "Don't you worry what happened to that little one?"

"Of course, how could I not worry? But there was no other way." She wiped at her cheeks, a wrinkle forming between her brows at Rapunzel's chastisement.

Rapunzel looked over her shoulder and nodded. Katterina emerged from the carriage, holding Helena. Helga looked at Rapunzel. "Have you had a child, my dear?"

"No, but I have found yours."

Helga cried out, stumbling backward and nearly falling. "No! I can't have her!"

Helena began to cry at the sudden scream.

Helga clutched at her belly and moaned, "Don't bring her over here, keep her far from me. You must leave! Leave now before the curse returns!"

Rapunzel stepped forward, hands outstretched as she pleaded, but Helga jerked backward again until Rapunzel stalled. "Helga, no, you needn't worry! The witch is dead, and the sorceress who commanded the witch is dead. I freed little Helena and another child at the same time. The other child is with his mother, and it is only right that she is now returned to you. We—we call her Helena, but you can change her name, of course."

Helga's eyes flooded with tears again, her work-worn hands holding her abdomen as though to shield the child growing there. "No! I can't have her, I gave her up for the good of all."

"But a daughter belongs with her mother."

"I will always love her, but if you bring her back, the babe in my womb will surely die. The children our family has had this last year will die."

"But—"

"You keep her!" She pointed violently at Paul. "You have a prince to care for her, so raise her in your castle far away.

Then I'll know she is safe and won't bring the curse back on us."

"But, Helga, you can't—" Paul put his arm around Rapunzel and turned her into his chest where she sobbed. She hiccuped and breathed in his musky scent. Why could she never cry without hiccuping? His strong hands rubbed her back as she cried herself dry. When she looked up, Helga had retreated inside and everyone had mounted their horses again. She stared at the door for a moment. As horrible as it was to think of losing Helena, how much more horrible would it be to one day tell her that her true mother didn't want her and considered her a curse? But there was nothing left to do.

Katterina came over to Rapunzel, still holding Helena, who was whimpering and rubbing her eyes with tight fists. "Your daughter." She spoke, her voice firm as she held out the wriggling babe who practically flung herself into Rapunzel's arms. "I'll saddle my horse."

THE NIGHT'S FIRE

The salty breeze that blew its twilight breath over the island as Edmund descended the gangplank was spiced with something he couldn't name. Was this the smell of the coffy bean King Tasufin had spoken of? There was something familiar and still unfamiliar about it. He had seen trees already in bloom, exotic colors brightening the landscape. The southern wind reportedly lent a mild winter to the archipelago of islands southwest of Alleria and the Eastern Ports. This left them the majority of the calendar to plant and harvest, plant and harvest. Every seventh year the islanders would leave their fields fallow, but this was not the year of rest. Judging by the laughter he heard weaving its way through the wind, tonight was not a night of rest either.

His father and mother were already on their way to the festivities, but he had lagged behind, tired of always feeling like he must accompany them somewhere. He had been on his own since he was sixteen, and though he had long wanted to be a part of a family, even his ties with the players had been loose and easily dissolved when it no longer suited him. He hungered now to be on his own again, searching out his own tales to sing, finding his own way in the world. He felt the frown pull his face down and tried to erase it. Would he ever be the kind of heir his father wanted? Despite the unfortunate discussion after meeting with King Tasufin, he pushed these thoughts away. Now was a time to revel, to have fun. Did he still remember how to do that?

Out of the corner of his eye, he caught a glimpse of Gwynndolen standing in the sand, staring hard at the mound the islanders were now unearthing. "What are they doing?" He leaned near her, breathing in her fresh fragrance. He smiled with humor; she must have cleaned up after caring for the horses that morning.

She startled at the sound of his voice and he noticed a blush fill her cheeks as her eyes darted to his. "Your Highness!"

He hated that! He was tired of everyone addressing him with such formality. He had longed to know his name most of his life. The baker had just called him "the boy," and his master who trained him to sing tales called him "troubadour." And now? He was never just *Edmund*. It was always *Your Highness* or *Prince Edmund*. "Call me Edmund."

As soon as he spoke the words, he wanted to snatch them back. Perhaps this was exactly the kind of behavior his father disapproved of. Gwynndolen looked dismayed, but he couldn't puzzle out why.

"I can't."

"Of course you can." He laughed at the utter ridiculousness of their situation. "You're a maid—a lady!—who can do nearly anything. I'm certain if you put your mind to it that you can call me simply 'Edmund.'"

She got that pursed look around her mouth that made him want to do something. He wasn't sure what. "It's not that I can't, *Your Highness*, it's that I shouldn't and therefore won't. It would dishonor your position."

He tilted his head to the side, her words flowing over him like a gentle breeze. She was saying something impassioned and likely had a point, but all he knew was that she looked lovely tonight. The flush in her cheeks had brightened her dark eyes, and her hair looked aflame. He really wanted to know what it felt like to touch her hair. Would it be hot? "Try it."

"What?"

"Try it. Say my name, just my name. No 'prince.' No 'Your Highness.' Go on—" He leaned in and lowered his voice. "There's no one around to hear you."

He thought she'd be angry, and perhaps he was even pushing her to get such a reaction, but instead she laughed out loud and glared at him with her odd sense of humor. "You are utterly impossible, *Edmund*."

"I'm glad to hear you know it." He contained himself and pointed to the coals the islanders were removing from the mounds. "What are they doing?" he asked again.

"Apparently, they buried several pigs and cooked them in beds of hot coals all day."

Was that the fragrance that he was smelling? He looked up and down the shore and admired how the workers were shoveling in time with the beat of a drum.

"I haven't been able to discover where the music is coming from."

Edmund smiled and offered his hand. "My Lady, let me show you."

Gwynndolen looked at his hand and then up into his face, her expression yielding like a flower unfolding. She placed her hand in his, and though he was not surprised by how small it was, he was startled by the callouses and the strength in her grip. He smiled; this woman was no frail flower. She was strength embodied.

He led her past several coal beds and stopped beside the

king and queen. There, before a great bonfire, was a massive drum. How large had the animal been whose dried skin now provided the head for the drum? The beat pulsed to his heartbeat, and he wished he had his lute. Wouldn't this be the perfect time to sing and play? But then he would have to relinquish Gwynndolen's hand, and for the moment she was content to be beside him. No, he didn't want his lute after all.

His eyes filmed over as he stared deeply into the flames. Flashes of his past came to him. His mother falling asleep. His abduction by the baker. The horrible things he had wished. The way he had betrayed Rapunzel, and what he had done after she left.

"Aren't you the prince?"

Edmund released Gwynndolen's hand and turned. The speaker was a wizened old woman, her unkempt, greasy grey-and-black hair hanging in lank locks around her pruned face as she hunched over her cane. His gaze narrowed as he nodded.

The old lady looked up at him. "No—open your eyes!"

He couldn't help being surprised at her command.

"Ah! Now I see who you be! The troubadour prince, living out one of your songs now, aren't you? Heading into danger, thataway." And with these garbled words, she pointed her bony chin to the northeast.

"Is it the tournament?" He had trouble speaking, his words sounding feeble, weak. "Will I be—" His voice dropped lest anyone should hear and think him a coward. "Will I be mortally wounded? Will I bring dishonor to my father?"

"Oh, the tournament, is that where you think a prince proves himself? No, it's on the way in the high seas, the choices he makes and then must live with."

He frowned. On the trip? The voyage would only take

another month or so, and all he had to do was to keep Camilla away and quit disappointing the king.

"I see you're having trouble with what I'm telling you, but it's all in your eyes, I can see it clear as anything. And what is imparted that is clear is the more to be feared. The Maker of us all will be calling on you to do what is right."

He nodded with a somber expression, though more confused than ever. "Of course—a prince and one-day king must always do what is right."

"No, Your Highness, not just nobility—a *man* must do right. And you've not learned that yet. You think if you just abstain and deny yourself, that is right. But the wish will get you, pull you back. You can't do it in your old self, in your own strength. You need Someone to work through you, make you a new man."

He tried to focus on her words, but they sounded more and more like gibberish. What was she saying, that he was a fool? That he was old? He needed to be young? Well, he wasn't exactly young, though he certainly felt so, having only just learned who he was and now swimming in all that was expected of him.

All at once, the drums stopped beating, and Edmund looked around him as though he had been in a trance. Where had the old woman gone? Servants were now bringing trays of meat to King Tasufin, who bowed to King Purnell and Queen Lefwenna to eat first.

Everyone ate standing up, grabbing chunks of meat from the platters with their bare fingers. It didn't burn as Edmund thought it should. How long had it taken for the servants to carve up the pigs? How long had Edmund been gazing at the fire, remembering things from his past, hearing from an old woman about his future? Gwynndolen glanced his way. "Are you quite well?" she asked, stepping closer.

He appreciated that she didn't use his formal title, though

he smiled as he noted she was out of hearing of the king and queen. He nodded while taking another bite, struggling again to swallow. "I think so."

She stared at him, as though he were a question she'd like the answer to. "I don't think so. Perhaps you should go lie down."

He laughed. How could he not? This maid didn't know him, and yet she could read him as few ever had. Not since Rapunzel . . . and Rapunzel had left. He felt something shift within him as he looked down at Gwynndolen. Did he want her to know him? To care?

The drums began beating again, and even though most were still eating, he grabbed Gwynndolen's hand.

"Edmund! What are you doing?"

He laughed as he ran with her to the group of islanders who had their hands clasped, dancing around the bonfire. They were whisked into the dance, which consisted mostly of circling the fire. There was distinct footwork involved, and he picked it up quickly, hoping that Gwynndolen would manage to do the same. She faltered a bit, but when he looked in her face, she didn't look angry, she looked elated. All at once the dancers were clapping, an intricate pattern that repeated until he and Gwynndolen picked it up. And then they were holding hands again and circling the fire. The dance continued in this way for a long time until it was done at last and the crowd onshore was clapping and laughing. Edmund turned to Gwynndolen, loving how her eyes were shining, perspiration curling the hair that touched her face. He held out his hand once more, and this time she took it without hesitation. He smiled full-out, with no thought of anything else—until he saw his father's face. Edmund dropped Gwynndolen's hand like a hot coal and stumbled back to his father.

"Did I do something wrong?"

"Do you think dancing like a common peasant becomes

an heir? If you were going to dance, it should have been with the princess of this island. That would have been an advantageous decision."

"But I was only—"

"Not thinking of your station again!" The king tried to lower his voice. "I wish you would take your role seriously." And with that, he turned away and headed back to the ship.

"Oh, Edmund . . ." the queen struggled, but could say no more and trailed after her husband.

Edmund stared at the ground, anger flooding his veins. Would he never get it right? The king had told him to discover what it meant to be a crown prince this summer, and all he could do was disappoint his father, his sovereign. Edmund turned away and walked away from the fires, as far as the island would let him go.

HIS

*P*aul awoke on the ground, aware that the fire had burned low. They had not put up the tents again because Rapunzel preferred to sleep in the open on clear nights. Not that they could see the sky very well, but they accommodated the princess when weather permitted.

The knight on watch was dozing, but he startled awake, seeing that his prince had noticed him. Very carefully, Paul looked around without making a noise. A snort caught him by surprise, and he realized it was his daughter who had woken him up. The little one had been resting between him and Rapunzel under the soft blankets. He could see her eyes were round even in the dim light. She was awake and wanting to play, evidently taking it into her head that grabbing a chunk of his hair was great fun. He slid out from between the blankets with Helena and walked a little way from the resting group, lighting a torch so that he could see where he was going. Was it his imagination, or did the Wood seem to grow darker each day? He tried to shake off the thought. Once out of hearing range, he set Helena down while he started a small fire and then sat cross-legged beside her.

Paul looked at the little girl as she pushed her rear end up into the air and grunted. She was *his*. He knew that Rapunzel felt deeply that there was something wrong now that they finally could call Helena their own, but he felt no misgiving. This little girl was now his, and he would do everything in his power to provide for her.

Helena bear-crawled over to take advantage of his knee, using it as a prop to pull herself up. Paul held out his fingers and she grasped them, getting her wobbly legs beneath her and pushing up into a standing position. Her little face beamed, surrounded by the dark cloud of fuzzy black hair that now covered her white scalp. He chuckled at her grin which revealed one little tooth peeking out of her bottom gum. If he let himself think of what she should be able to do at her age, he might grow sad at all that was stolen from her. But he caught those thoughts and stared at her. Even if she was late at crawling, at teething, he would love her all the same. "I promise you this, little one: I will not expect you to be like anyone else. You've had a hard time of it so far, but now you have us.

"We will always fight for you, till the day we die. You have a family now, to help you grow and to pray for your strength. Together, we will laugh and help you to know how good this life can be. You will grow in wisdom as you learn of our Savior. It is true, you may not have been born to us, but you are ours, and we will never let you go."

The little girl's fathomless eyes reflected the dancing light of the flames. Those eyes stared into his as though she could grasp his serious oath. Then she bobbed and crumpled, her little legs no longer able to hold her up. She bumped down on her bottom with a mystified gurgle. "But you did so well!" Paul laughed. "You were able to stay up so much longer than last time!" Still, she scrunched up her little face in frustration and reached for his fingers again to haul herself back up onto unsteady feet.

"She won't give up, will she?" Katterina's voice came from behind him.

"Is everyone waking?"

The woman still moved with the grace and silence of a cat on the prowl. "I don't know about everyone. Your wife is still dreaming."

"Is she smiling?" Paul looked over his shoulder at his mother-in-law.

"She does look like she is smiling."

"Good." He looked back at Helena, who was bouncing with excitement. "Then she will come to accept our good fortune."

"What do you mean?" Katterina sat down across from him and held out her fingers to Helena, who moved as though she would cross to her grandmother, but then landed on her bottom with a snort of frustration.

"She has had a few nightmares since we left Dorothea's, even after Helga gave us Helena."

Katterina was silent for a moment, thinking. "Losing Dorothea was hard, but I think it's more than that. I think Rapunzel feels afraid, maybe that she doesn't deserve to be Helena's mother."

Paul held out his fingers to the determined little girl, but he felt his face scrunch up in a frown. "But that's what she wanted."

"It may be what she wanted, but she never expected to receive it."

"And now that she has?"

Katterina gave one shoulder a lift. "She is struggling. But I think it is only for a time. She will soon accept the joy of raising this little one as your own."

Paul nodded and stared again into the eyes of his daughter. "I think her eyes are purple."

"I think you're right!"

He smiled up at this woman, his wife's mother and his friend. "I was thinking that I had been imagining that. Anytime I have said anything to Rapunzel, she has told me they are deep blue."

"No, they really are purple. Why do you think Rapunzel wouldn't want to see that?"

"I don't know."

"Our Rapunzel is a little odd, it's true. Of course, it's my fault she is the way she is."

"She forgave you." Now that Helena was standing up again with his help, he moved closer to Katterina, encouraging the little girl to reach for her grandmother.

"I know, but that doesn't erase the effects of her strange upbringing, does it?" Katterina reached with her fingers, and the little girl grunted, narrowing her eyes as she reached.

"And I love her all the more for it."

"What kind of queen do you think she will make?" Helena finally let go of Paul, and they both gave a quiet "Hurrah!" when the little one teetered closer and closer to Katterina's lap.

"A thoughtful one. A cautious one. But still, one who laughs and loves the life she's been given."

"That's what I think, too. She will be the kind of queen that our people will appreciate."

Helena looked over her shoulder, back at her father.

"But . . .?" Katterina prompted, simultaneously turning Helena around to make her journey back to Paul.

"But?"

"Yes, you sounded as though at some point you were bound to say, 'But . . .'"

Paul lifted out his fingers just a little further away this

time, to make Helena reach. "But—I don't think *she* believes she can be a proper queen. Because of her upbringing. Because of how misadventure follows her."

Katterina laughed and dropped her hands into her lap as Helena triumphantly crossed over. "I can see how that might cause worry for her. Perhaps she needs to study the kings and queens of old. They were either dreadfully boring or always causing problems, if I remember right."

"You remember well."

"So, she just needs an adjustment of her expectations, doesn't she? And who doesn't need such an adjustment after receiving the gift of a child or a husband or a kingdom? And she's had all three in the space of less than a year."

Paul lifted Helena high in the air to make her giggle and then blew noisily onto her belly. He laughed at her laughter and then looked back at Katterina. "But you say my wife really was smiling in her sleep?"

"That I did."

"Then it will work out. We'll just trust God to work his will." Paul took a deep breath and snuggled his daughter. He wished God would hurry his will along.

THE PIRATES' VOW

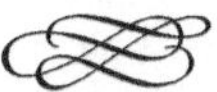

Camilla was tired of waiting. That's what she felt she
had been doing for years. Waiting and waiting. First
for Ute to connect the sisters, then to make certain her sacrifices were ripe before she offered them. And now? She was
simply waiting for the prince to fall.

Beneath the ship in the dark waters she began to circle,
knowing the stress this would cause for the crew. If she
circled again and again, it could eventually spin the ship. Her
laughter shot up toward the surface. Maybe it was time to do
something, to cause Edmund to make a choice. She couldn't
keep waiting forever, she needed to find a way—what would
Ute do? She grimaced, wishing again that her sister was still
alive. She had to find a way to Amee—all the sacrifices had
to mean something, and Ute's death had to be avenged!

With her mind she reached out, exploring boundaries.
How close could she get now? Oh! How delightful! She could
reach all the way to the black shores of the Land of
Midnight, past the archipelago, but she could not travel any
further east on the southern coast of Alleria. Amee was still
beyond her. If they could only make contact! Then she could

make certain things were still intact. The plan could still work. It had changed, now that Ute was no longer alive to see it through, but the essence was still there.

Something beckoned her. On the periphery of her senses, she could—well, she could almost smell change. There was a ship, a special ship. She stopped her circling and sped through the deep waters to the east. How far was it? Just at the edge of her limits? Perfect. She rose above the waters, allowing her powers to transform her breathing so that she could suck in great gulps of air once her head emerged above the calm sea.

There. She saw the dark ship with its black sails. The Land of Midnight on a ship. A woman was standing watch on board with a stony face and skin so dark that only the whites of her eyes were visible by moonlight.

"How many of you are there?"

The woman started, but to her credit, didn't scream. Camilla saw the flash of her teeth as she spoke: "What are you?"

Oh, how Camilla did enjoy this game! "You have heard of me, I'm sure. I am known to your people, and you are bound to do what I say."

"But I don't trust my eyes. I've stood at watch too long tonight."

"That may be so, but it does not change the fact that you are conversing with a leviathan."

The woman was not to be cowed into believing. "There are a great many things that my people have believed in years past. I do well to question my eyes before deciding you are the one we are bound to. After all, you could just be the product of an overly imaginative mind."

"Was it imagination that freed your people from the plague not so long ago?" Camilla opened her mouth and smacked her lips together. "Don't you remember how just a few of your people came to me in the sea to ask for help? I set you free, did I not?"

"If it was truly you."

"Who else could it be?"

"As I've said, you could be the product of an overly imaginative mind. A captain should always be on guard."

"Oho! *A captain?* A captain who takes the night watch!"

"I am not just the captain, I am also a sailor. I know the waters we traverse are hostile to our kind. We take turns, all of us, on the night watches."

Camilla liked the middle-aged woman. She would have been but a child when Camilla gave a small crew the cure to end the plague—and made them promise to roam the waters as pirates fetching things: information for her, loot for themselves. "But you are my pirate, are you not?"

The captain raised her eyebrows; this woman did not like to be reminded of her people's servitude. "My people have done what we must to rebuild our country. I admit, you seem to be the one we serve."

"How long have you been in the waters, captain?"

"Long enough I would have thought I'd have met you by now."

Camilla tilted her head to see the woman from another angle. Yes, she would do nicely. "I wasn't able to go far till recently."

The captain nodded. "I suppose that shouldn't surprise me—otherwise, why would you have needed us?"

"I chose to use you—I need no one."

"Then, you will let us go without further delay?"

Camilla laughed at this. "I am a shape-shifting sorceress, and you are bound to me. You are not free to go till you and your crew have served me. I have use for a pirate and her crew."

"Will it benefit us? Besides not being eaten by you, of course."

Camilla laughed again. "I know where a treasure is."

There was a beat, a hesitation of interest that made Camilla's greedy heart pound. "Oh, yes?"

"In the coffers of King Purnell. His ship is coming this way."

"I like treasure."

"I thought you might."

The pirate's voice tightened, suspicious. "Why can't you do this yourself?"

"It's more fun this way, and your people owe me. In order to get the treasure, though, you must do exactly as I say."

"And what would that be?"

"Kill the royal family, but leave the prince alive."

TRAIN WITH A FOOL

*A*mis followed Dietz, who had wandered deeper into the Wood while following Prince Paul and Jacob on a rest day. The young man crouched behind a huge fern, peering at the men as they trained, metal clashing on metal as they took turns defending and advancing. Quieter than most people would guess he could, the fool crept up behind Dietz and whispered in his ear, "What are you doing?"

Dietz flung himself back, and Amis laughed harder than he had in a fortnight. Paul and Jacob found him holding his sides while the young man sulked nearby.

"What are the two of you up to?"

Amis wiped the tears from his eyes. "I was having a bit of fun at the young man's expense, I'm afraid. There was no harm meant, Dietz."

Paul and Jacob sheathed their swords, having surmised there was no physical threat. "Amis . . ." Paul said with a scowl.

"I know, I know!" He held up his hands in surrender; he must have gone too far for good-tempered Paul to look like that. "It was probably too much."

"Dietz, why were you following us?"

Dietz shrugged, his face still lowered to the ground.

The two warriors exchanged a glance, and Paul looked at Amis with a twinkle in his eye. "I think the young man needs a chance to prove himself. And you, my overreaching fool, shall provide such a chance."

Amis stood up and brushed himself off. How to play this? "Of course, if it pleases Your Highness."

"It does. Have you a weapon?"

Amis shook his head. "Only my wit."

"We all know that left you before you came following Dietz."

Amis nodded with a lift of his shoulder.

"And you, Dietz, do you have a weapon of choice?"

"I was only taught to use magic against people, but I don't want to now. Oh, and a bow and arrow."

Jacob walked over to a tree where weapons were propped for Paul's training. He grabbed a staff in each hand, tossing one to Amis and the other to the young man. "Amis, come, let's teach Dietz some of the basics of using a staff."

Amis was well acquainted with the staff but preferred a dagger. He didn't like anything large that impeded his ability to jump, flip, and run. Then again—he planted the staff in the ground and used it to vault himself next to the young man.

"Amis! He's not ready for that."

It was a shame there were so many rules to follow when teaching weaponry. Amis settled himself for the lesson and tried to concentrate.

⚬⚬⚬

GWYNNDOLEN WAS through with being ignored. Seeing that the prince was once more training on deck with her brothers, she strapped on her sword and waited for her chance. Soon, Liam had Edmund pinned up against the port bow, and Liam elbowed him in the face. The prince dropped his sword. Gwynndolen, lithe as always, fetched it and tossed it back to him before Liam could snatch it up. They had taken Liam by surprise, but Georgius came around, forcing them to travel aft toward amidships. Standing side by side, they fought back as the brothers advanced. But the brothers split to attack one-on-one. "Back-to-back!" Gwynndolen shouted, and they were soon fighting off the brothers with their backs protected. "Strike hard!" she crowed, striking Georgius's hand and then pointing the tip of her sword at his chest. Edmund front-kicked Liam as payback for being elbowed. He had his sword at Liam's throat before he could blink.

"We yield! We yield!" The brothers laughed and then re-sheathed their swords when Gwynndolen and the prince gave them room.

"Well done!" the queen said, clapping her hands. Gwynndolen hadn't seen her watching, as her focus had been entirely on her brothers and the prince. "My dears, you were magnificent! What a great team you make." Gwynndolen wiped away the perspiration from her brow and beamed at Edmund, only then realizing he was not pleased. In fact, he looked crushed. "Son, why are you upset?" she heard his mother ask.

The prince shook his head. "It's nothing, mother."

The queen glanced behind and saw the king at the same time that Gwynndolen saw him. He looked at Edmund and shook his head, then made for the lower decks.

Gwynndolen looked at the prince. His bright eyes had dimmed, and he couldn't meet her gaze. She had made it worse, somehow, hadn't she?

She started for the lower decks when the queen reached for her. "He still needs you, my dear."

"He doesn't need me. He needs his father. The king doesn't approve of what you want for us, does he?"

"The king wants what's best for Rona. I know that to be you. Give Edmund time—he will do what's right."

"And what is right? I've not said I want to be queen. I doubt I'll even make a good lady at court."

"You will stand by his side while he takes his place. I've already asked him to protect you—"

"Protect me? I don't need protecting!"

"At court, my dear, he will look after you. You may be better with a horse and a sword, for now, but he handles people quite well."

"Except the king."

"The king will not be handled. But it's no matter, the king will come around as he sees for himself what a great team you shall be."

Gwynndolen could only shake her head at her aunt. Did the woman understand nothing?

A CURSE OR A BLESSING?

*E*dmund wasn't sure what to do with the hand on his shoulder beneath the bright sun reflecting off of the endless waters. Although he could tell that Georgius was aware of his discomfort, the broad man didn't back off.

"Your Highness, it might be wrong of me to say, but I think of you as a brother. I know you to be a man of character, even if you do not know this of yourself. True, you have made mistakes in the past and have much to learn, but don't you know? We would follow you to the gate of hell. When you become king—"

"I doubt my father will allow me to be his heir. Not when what he desires me to do—" But Edmund couldn't speak of what he'd done. Not to this good-natured brother-at-arms who trusted him.

"Whatever happened in the past will stay there—"

Edmund shook his head in frustration. "I know you mean well, Georgius, but the truth is more painful than that. Each action we take, every decision we make has far-reaching consequences. What I've done has shaped me, and there's no way I can escape it." He could feel in his bones the very weight of each selfish wish. He could even feel the cost of the wishes he had made to help others. The image of the baker's wife, Cibel, clung to him. The vision of the maid Plesencia's brother was ever before him. His hands were stained crimson; he could never wash them free of the blood. Though he didn't want to think about it, he saw Rapunzel's face as she declared herself free from him, making her choice to embrace her own liberty. But he had put her through so much, as he was afraid of doing now to Gwynndolen. Even now—perhaps especially now—he knew he would never be free.

Georgius shook him, though perhaps not as hard as he should have. Edmund knew he was being difficult. "Think, man, you need not be a slave any longer. There is freedom available for you. Freedom for all of us. A new beginning, a fresh start. Wasn't that what you were looking for when you came to find your family?"

"But I didn't find a new beginning, I discovered a long chain of events that made me the way I am, forever linked to the past. There is now no way to break free and become the man I want to be."

"You think of your past mistakes like a curse, a curse instead of a blessing. But couldn't it be the blessing you've always wanted? What if there was a way to reverse things? I think God is stronger than anything that binds you—I know he is! He uses even what is horrible and transforms it for those who love him. I remember it says in the holy scriptures that there is nothing that can separate us from the love of God. It also says that he works all things together for the good of those who are called according to his purpose. Think on that, my prince!

"I've known others who think the way you do, as though they are trapped by the bad decisions they or others have made. But those who think like that perish. My father was poisoned for years because we trusted someone we shouldn't have. We could spend what's left of his life bemoaning that fact. I could spend all of my time as the next lord rueing what I didn't see—what I didn't do for him. But there's another way. I choose to treasure what I have left with him. In our family, we have grown stronger even in the midst of our suffering. He has asked me, when I return home, to officially take my place as lord. And I will —not because I have to, but because I want to serve him, to serve you, to live the way I can with what I have. I will marry my beloved and become a good husband by the grace of God."

"How can you know that?"

"Because I know myself—I know the man God has made me to be, and I will do my best with what I have. We are all living under a curse, you know."

"What do you mean?" Edmund stiffened.

"The first man who walked in the garden with God betrayed him. He chose to do the one thing God asked him not to do. In a land of plenty, he gave in to his temptation and ate the forbidden fruit his wife handed him. He should have chosen wisely. He should have protected his wife and all of creation. But he didn't, and we live in a fallen world because of him. But we also now have a Savior who came to set things right."

"You are talking of Jesu, God's Son."

"Have you taken your problem to him?"

Edmund shook his head. Why would he bring to God a problem he had made worse and worse? He should be able to fix this on his own.

"You are not alone in your fight. Perhaps we could all learn to take such things to God. What if I had only taken my misgivings about my father's health to God . . .? But that's in the past, now, isn't it? I will make mistakes going forward, my prince. But that won't stop me from receiving grace every day to live the best I can."

"You're different from me. You were raised in a family to learn how to live right—"

"Make whatever excuses you must, but they won't help you change and become the man you are destined to become."

"What man is that?"

"A man who would sacrifice his own well-being, his very life, to care for those he loves, those he has vowed to protect and serve."

The moment hung heavy and full of promise. But perhaps not. What did Georgius know of sorcery and wishes? What did he know of pain, pain that made Edmund's bones ache? No one understood the choices he had made to save people, choices that were twisted to hurt the very ones the prince was devoted to.

He tallied the wishes made for others—so many. To travel. To free his mother. To bring the baker to justice. To make people forget Plesencia so he could save Rapunzel's life.

The selfish ones—creating his pink playmate, and engraving her on his lute when he couldn't take her from make-believe to the real world. Wishing Rapunzel into making her travel with him; wishing Rapunzel to marry him. All the wishes for the baker he had made because he was more afraid of the baker's punishment than of the pain the wish brought. So many evil wishes.

And the failed wish—to win a hunt and thereby earn his father's approval. He had been foolish to think it would cost so little.

No wonder Camilla had grown in power once he returned to Rona. So many wishes, so much pain. He had been wrong. Even when he meant well, it had gone wrong.

THE DANCE

Katterina went off by herself again after supper, but this time Jacob followed. He let her take her time meandering beneath the dark trees, but when he realized she might keep going and hadn't noticed him following, he spoke. "My Lady?"

She turned to him, and he was grateful for the last bit of light to see her lovely face. Her bright green eyes were veiled, but he didn't know why. "Jacob . . ."

His name sounded strange, as though there was something that she wanted to say to him but didn't know how. "You seem preoccupied."

She wrapped her arms around herself. He stepped near to place his cloak around her shoulders, but she didn't look up at him. Was she angry?

"Katter—Lady Katterina, surely we know one another well enough by now that you trust me."

"I do trust you, Jacob, but I think that's the problem."

His chest squeezed at the look on her face as she turned from him. "I'm sorry, but I don't know what I've done to offend you."

"It's not you, it's me. I—" With this, she turned back to him, but struggled to speak. She cleared her throat and then gave a brief laugh. "Do you know?" she asked at last, a sly grin covering her features. "I think sometimes that my life as a cat was easier than my life as a human. There are all these rules to what one can and cannot do. I wasn't raised to life as a lady, never really wanted it, but if I want to be a part of my daughter's life, here I am. There are many things in this world that say how you must live, how you should speak, how you should act with different people—" She licked her lips. "For instance, I enjoy our talks. I love my daughter, Paul, and little Helena, but it's been wonderful having someone nearer my age who understands the world."

He nodded, waiting.

She let her eyes fall. "But, it's not right, is it?"

"My Lady?"

"A warrior monk and a widow—a widow who was once a cat used by a witch! You've been removed from your people for so long, but now we are returning. Do you think our friendship will be well-received by the order? By the Father?"

Is that what she was worried about? He gave a dry laugh that made him cough. "My Lady, there is no hard and fast rule that says I can't befriend a widow. And I would speak strong words against any who would argue that with me."

She measured him with her gaze. "I think you'll see things differently when you are back in the presence of your brothers."

"You think I've grown lax, being so far from them?"

A crease appeared between her eyebrows. "No! Of course not. You are the most disciplined person I've ever met. No, I simply think that you were a young man when you left and you had strong ideas of what was required of you. You've said you made a choice to hold the order above other pursuits, personal relationships—"

"And I've since regretted that decision."

"But there was a reason you decided that. There was a reason the young man, fresh from his training, made that choice."

"So you *do* think I've grown lax."

"I think you may change your mind back, and if so, I want you to know that I understand. The order is a lifelong pursuit."

"God is my lifelong pursuit. The order of monks raised me. It's all I've ever known."

At this, she simply stared at him. Moments went by, the noises from the company bedding down for the night filtering through the trees. At last she spoke. "And now?"

"And now, I don't regret the life I've had, but I would choose differently, had I to do things over."

"But you can't do things over."

"No, but there is scripture that reminds us that each new day brings fresh hope for beginning again. Just as you have begun again. I'm a man of my word, and I want to understand *how* to continue to be with my new understanding of who God is."

Katterina's laughter lifted his heart as her eyes crinkled. "We're always dancing, you and I. Never quite saying all we mean."

"I'd like to speak more clearly, but I can't yet."

"I know. Good night, Jacob."

"Good night, Katterina."

THE SEA SERPENT

The ship began rolling before daybreak. It felt as though it were literally sloshing back and forth. Gwynndolen could barely stand up, but she was grateful her stomach was sturdy, unlike that of Beatrix, who had turned a pale shade of green and began emptying the contents of her stomach immediately. She knew she should stay with her sister, or perhaps check on her brothers, but her chief concern was below. She carefully made her way lower and lower into the bowels of the ship. There she found the horses tossing their heads, only upright because of the slings that wrapped them tight. She tried to calm them down but felt lost as to how to make their situation better.

She remained below, though, and Georgius found her there and begged her to come up on deck. It must have been midafternoon by then, but she would never have known it to be so by the dark growling sky she could see through the hatch, sky that crackled with thunder and lit with jagged streaks of lightning. Her brother put his face to her ear to speak. "The prince insists you join him!" he yelled above the sound of the waves crashing against the sides of the ship.

"But why?"

"I don't know!" He held tight to her hand as they climbed through the hatch.

The prince was standing by the rail. Next to him, a great, eel-like monster reared her head from the waves and rasped into the air the words Gwynndolen had feared:

"You can't save him. You can try, dear girl, but you can't save someone as lost as your poor prince. He was promised to me long ago and has made his destiny worse, wish by wish. It's time that he comes to know this about himself, that there is no hope for him, and there has never been any for you."

"Who are you? *What* are you?"

"I'm just someone who speaks the truth and lures men to their doom." Her throaty cackle felt like thunder in Gwynndolen's ears. "Wouldn't you say that's an honest assessment of who I am, Your Highness?"

Edmund's eyes, so blank before, suddenly filled with black ink, as though the pupils of each eye had grown to cover the entire thing. He nodded blankly. "I gave myself to her, wish by wish, and now I am her servant."

"My slave!" She opened her huge maw wide and leaned down to touch her chin to the side of the rail.

Edmund turned from Gwynndolen and climbed inside the mouth. It clipped shut over his form, the sound of breaking bones and the squish of torn flesh filling the air even more loudly than the thunder.

And then, there was darkness.

Full, complete darkness, accompanied by empty silence.

Gwynndolen shook herself and woke up. She had been dreaming. The sea was calm, at least for now.

Beatrix moaned in bed beside her. "What are you about?"

"Nothing," Gwynndolen whispered as she tried to ease

herself out of bed. She hadn't had nightmares since her father first became ill. Why now? "Go back to sleep."

"Mmmmm?" Gwynndolen could see the little frown between Beatrix's brow crease and then relax by the small amount of light pouring through the tiny porthole. She located her cotehardie and surcoat and quickly rebraided her hair from the mess it had become in her sleep. It was easier than brushing it out. She opened the door a smidge and looked out. Darkness filled the corridor, and she had to wait a moment while her eyes adjusted. She knew which way to go, but she wanted to be certain she was stepping correctly, or she knew her unsettled spirit would have her stumbling into walls.

After carefully making her way topside, she found Edmund by the side of the ship, speaking to that *thing* from her nightmares. Gwynndolen was fully awake this time. She could feel the cool night on her skin, smell the salt of the frothing sea. She was no longer dreaming. This was real: the prince was consorting with a monster of some sort.

The creature's pale eyes, each as large as Gwynndolen's whole head, narrowed and looked at her as she let out a great hiss. "It seems we have company again, my prince."

Turning with nonchalance, he stared at her—or was it through her? What had happened to the carefree prince who had insisted she call him *Edmund*? Where was the man who had grabbed her hands and led her to dance? Why was he now looking at her like that, as though she were an annoyance?

"What is she?" Gwynndolen hated the tremor in her voice.

Edmund scowled and walked forward, grabbing her pointing finger and taking her hand in his. "Return to bed, Lady Gwynndolen. You are exhausted, there is nothing up here you need concern yourself with."

"Oh, no? Not even a leviathan threatening our lives?"

He blinked and looked down at her. She thought for a moment that his eyes would fill to the brim with black. But his bruised expression pricked her heart. A great splash shook the ship and he jerked forward, his head colliding with Gwynndolen's.

The coarse voice thundered. "That's one way to make an impression on a young lady, Your Highness."

Both Gwynndolen and Edmund rubbed their heads. "I'm sorry," he said, his voice lowering.

"I'm not sorry." She hoped her voice didn't really sound that weak to the other two listening. "I just know that you shouldn't be up here alone with that—that thing!"

"If I leave her, I don't know what she'll do."

Gwynndolen pushed her way past Edmund, refusing to allow fear to stop her. "What are you here for?"

"Me? Oh, your prince knows very well. I'm here for him. He belongs to me—and you already know it, don't you, little lady?"

"I don't know any such thing. Edmund belongs to the royal household, he's a member of the church, he's—"

"Being a member of the church doesn't save someone when they were first promised to me. He has certain powers. Haven't you heard?"

Gwynndolen scowled, but had to nod. "He told me so himself, but he can choose God's way instead."

Camilla's tentacle waved away her reference to God as she leaned closer. "How very interesting. You must mean something to him. Has he tried to wish you to do something as he did with that other maid?"

"No—but even if he tried, he wouldn't get very far with me."

Camilla's thundering laughter split the air. "You don't

think so? You might be right, as there are a few who can resist. The prince learned that the hard way last winter."

"No, it was around harvest, not winter, that Rapunzel broke through the spell of his wish."

"No, my dear, not Rapunzel. The brother—Plesencia's brother? Oh, wait! This is fun! Edmund, you've only told half your story. How many people don't know?"

His eyes lowered. "My mother and my father know."

"But not this lady who means so much to you?"

Edmund was now shaking his head.

"Oh, then I think I'll leave you two to chat for a time. I'll make certain that the watch stays fast asleep a bit longer while you do."

TOO CLOSE

Gwynndolen caught her hand on the side of the ship as the great creature lowered her form and caused the whole vessel to bob in the water. How could no one else wake with such rocking? Was the monster really so powerful? She turned to face the prince, words sharp in the night air: "What have you been hiding from me?"

Edmund reached out, touching her braid and holding it. "I knew it would burn."

"What?"

"You, getting close to you. You have to know everything, don't you?"

"No." She watched him coil his finger in the curl at the tail of the braid. "I don't have to know *everything*. But this— this is obviously—" But she couldn't finish the thought. He had sunk into himself, the same expression that had masked his face after he had danced with her and disappointed his father. As much as she hated being lied to, even by omission, Gwynndolen found she was hurting for the pain that was etched into each crevice of his face. "What is it?"

"There was a maidservant of Rapunzel's last summer."

"I don't remember her having—"

"By the time we came to your father's lands, the girl was dead and forgotten."

"Forgotten? I don't understand."

"The witch had cast some sort of spell over a love potion in a pendant that had been gifted to Rapunzel by the High Queen. Wanting to honor Plesencia, her maidservant, Rapunzel gave it to her. But the spell had changed it to poison, and it killed the girl. Rapunzel was accused of her murder, and I used my gift of wish to set her free."

Gwynndolen blinked. "How?"

"I wished for no one to remember her—no one but myself and Rapunzel. All seemed well. I mean, the wish cost me, as all wishes do. Now I know it strengthened Camilla." He paused, dark eyes scrutinizing her face. "Gwynndolen, I thought I was saving Rapunzel, that she would love me for it."

"And did she?"

"I think she feared me for it. She worried over what kind of king I would be with such power."

Gwynndolen nodded to encourage him to finish. She would hold off on judging; she knew there was more to the tale.

"Well, you know what happened. Rapunzel made her choice and left me. But during the winter, Plesencia's brother"—Edmund's brow lowered as his lips tightened—"somehow came awake. He remembered his older sister— missed her. I remember the feeling I would get sometimes. I'd look around and see him watching me. He became sullen. He had been a happy little page, but no longer.

"One night, in the dead of winter, he burst into our Great Hall. He came at me, a lad of eleven or twelve years, and tried to slit my throat. I needed no assistance in disarming him. He was screaming for his sister—that I, the mysterious prince, had bewitched everyone but him. I told the truth of what had happened to Plesencia, even though my mother and father couldn't remember her. There was no consoling the lad—he slit his throat before us. It was my fault! His blood spilled over my hands when I tried to stop him."

Gwynndolen shuddered.

"I wanted to make a wish right then, to change things and make them better for his family, but—I wished everyone outside my presence would forget him. And just like that, I blotted him out of existence."

"But you didn't, not completely. Your parents remember him."

Edmund shook his head. "Even that was a mistake, I fear, for now my father knows what I'm capable of and thinks I could use the power to help the kingdom."

Gwynndolen shook her head, but she couldn't clear her mind so easily. "And how does this tie you to—to that thing?" She stared out into the night where Camilla had taunted them moments before.

"Each time I wish, it strengthens her. I didn't know until she met with my mother and me on the shores of Maer. But each time that I've made a wish since returning to Rona, it has given her more and more power. Even now, while at sea, she stays near and garners power."

"Who is she?" Though the question was said, Gwynndolen already knew the answer.

"One of the sisters of sorcery."

"And if you continue to wish while near her, then she will become what she was in our grandparents' time?"

"Yes."

"*This* is why the queen—" Edmund looked confused, and Gwynndolen stopped her words before revealing the queen's proposal. She blinked, struggling. "But surely, the king knows the cost . . .?"

Edmund just stared into her eyes, and she knew. The king didn't count the cost the same way. "My father does not think the sisters would bring the war back to our shore. They didn't before, and he feels it might even create an opportunity to come out from under the High King's thumb."

There were no words she could think to say. The way before them was darker than she could have ever imagined. "Edmund, how will you ever—wait. Why are you smiling?"

"You called me 'Edmund.'"

She shrugged, but her cheeks burned. "You told me to."

"I know, but after the way that night ended . . ." He let his voice trail off, the bit of amusement wiped from his features.

"What does the king want from you?"

"To take my role seriously. To use my wish for the kingdom. To not act like the troubadour I was."

What could she say? There was nothing. "Edmund, I'm sorry."

A sad smile lifted his features and he dropped her braid, reaching out to cup her face. "I wish—" and his mouth shut tight before he turned to go belowdecks.

THE DWELLING

Rapunzel was already tired when she saw that they were coming up on a dwelling of some sort. It wasn't unusual to discover grand homes along the way, but she had not recently seen anything this elaborate built so far from a market town. The carriage creaked to a halt, unsettling birds from their branches. She was grateful to dismount her gelding and stretch her legs, leading the horse to a nearby stream. Unlike Dorothea's cottage, the huge house was not in a clearing. In fact, the trees grew closer together, if that was possible, branches overlapping one another, gaps in the leaves allowing in a grey, weak light by which to see. Her mother had no trouble getting out of the carriage and avoiding tree roots, but Rapunzel found traversing the ground difficult. She happily relieved her mother of Helena and placed the wriggling toddler on her hip, but she trod deliberately to avoid tree roots as she carried the small, burbling mass of energy.

The horses clomped over to the stream, led by knights in clinking chain mail, Amis and Dietz helping. Had the area been quiet and peaceful before their arrival? It was hard to tell now. Jacob went to the door of the building. The road that led here had been well-traveled, but the courtyard, if the small space could be called that, proved the estate had few occupants and fewer visitors. It was sturdy, but the thick vines growing up the sides and the trees crowding in suggested it had not been a home for many years. Jacob was cautious as he approached the ornate, massive doors on the prince's behalf. Rapunzel tried to quell the irrational fear growing in her. Moments passed as they waited for someone, anyone to answer the door. Nothing happened. At last, Jacob walked over to Paul.

"My prince, I believe it would be best if I took a few knights and we looked over the place to ascertain if it would be safe to stay here."

Paul nodded his assent, but insisted he go as well. Rapunzel smiled. Her husband would never be the sort of ruler who expected others to do what he himself was capable of.

Helena babbled and reached toward a thin shaft of light that broke through the oppressing deepness. Would the poor child go blind, spending all this time in the Wood? Rapunzel hoped they would find relief from the darkness soon, and was grateful when a knight lit a lamp that hung by the doors.

They stood still and waited, and waited, and continued to wait. Helena's impatience at being held grated. Rapunzel set her down at last and let the little one get her energy out, exploring the gnarled roots sticking up all over the ground. Helena's little bottom shot up in the air as she moved in her typical bear-crawl. Would she never get down on her knees? After a moment, Rapunzel squatted down beside her daughter, holding out her fingers to help the child practice walking. Helena snorted and laughed in glee. For a solitary moment, Rapunzel was filled with a deep sense of satisfaction.

A shriek pierced the air. Rapunzel scooped up Helena and held her close. It was so dark, even with the lamp lit, that she couldn't be sure she should trust her eyes. The horses by the stream stomped and neighed uneasily.

"Princess Rapunzel, get behind me!" A knight used his body as a shield, and Rapunzel felt the rough bark of a tree behind her. She raised on tiptoe to peer over the knight's shoulder. Good—even in the dim light, she could see another knight shielding Katterina. Stillness fell over the Wood. Amis had settled the horses, and not an animal stirred. Even Helena seemed to hold her breath.

Rapunzel thought she saw something move near the ground, but was it her imagination? She peered into the shadows just past the knight's shoulder, wincing when another shriek sent shivers up her spine.

"Rapunzel?" came Katterina's voice. "What are you seeing?"

A mist crawling low to the ground began to rise. It formed a cloud shaped like a long, stringy man. His eyes, if Rapunzel wasn't imagining him, were long and hollow, his mouth a yawning chasm. "A man made of fog?"

"I see him, too." Katterina sounded as though she had made a decision. "Let me by."

"My Lady?" asked the knight.

"I must speak to him." The knight tried to argue, but there was steel in her voice. "You must stand aside."

Rapunzel's throat was dry, and she bit back her argument. Perhaps it was time she trusted her mother. Katterina stepped forward, her voice steady. "What do you want?"

"Only to see with my eyes who is coming this way." The man's voice was a deep baritone, thick with the accent Rapunzel had come to know was from the Eastern Ports.

"This way? What way is that?" Katterina's voice was calm. How often had she had to stay calm in order to do the witch's bidding when she had been Cat? Katterina may have changed forms, but obviously she still knew how to deal with things emanating evil.

The man seemed to laugh, but Rapunzel couldn't be sure. The sound was that of a clogged bellows used at a forge to stoke a fire.

Katterina was not deterred. "What way is that?" she repeated.

"To the marsh, of course, to meet my mistress."

Rapunzel tried to step forward, but her knight pushed her back. Rapunzel felt helpless, but that didn't really matter now; what mattered was the threat at hand. "What do you want?" she called out.

"I don't want anything but for my mistress to be happy. And now that we have found you tripping over our roots on your way, we will gladly welcome you."

"Who are you?"

"You will meet me soon enough, and when you do, all will be revealed. The men think they have a tournament to fight in, but it is time for war." His form disintegrated, a vapor gone before Rapunzel could grasp his meaning. As he disappeared, Paul came around the corner with Jacob. Was it her imagination, or had the lamp grown brighter since the apparition dissolved?

"Did you find anyone?" Rapunzel's knight allowed her to walk over to Paul. She reached out to touch him, her heart fearing until she could feel for herself that he was solid.

"No, the entire place is abandoned, though I can't see why. There is food in the Great Hall, freshly prepared as though they knew we were on our way, and the bedrooms are ready for guests. There are no animals in the stables, though. I just don't know what to make of it." He reached to take Helena from Rapunzel's arms.

Jacob joined them, and the women spoke of what they had seen, the knights nodding along.

"Is it wise to stay in a place clearly infused with magic?"

A dark-skinned woman materialized from the shadows. "We welcome you."

THE SONG

Rapunzel gasped as Jacob stepped forward, staff in hand. Paul handed off Helena to take his stance among the knights. "Who are you? Where did you just come from?"

"I've been here all along." The woman's words were Allerian, but clipped, as though she had to speak very distinctly or risk being misunderstood. Rapunzel noted the coarse brown tunic she wore and concluded she was a nun. Several more women stepped forward to stand near her, some with pale skin and hair, others dark like her, but each one dressed the same. They bowed their heads in reverence, and Jacob answered them in turn.

"Why could we not see you?"

"Because light and darkness cannot coexist. You must have either one or the other. I would have thought you knew that, having known Dorothea."

"How do you know of our dealings in the Dark Wood?"

"We are the Ladies of the Light. We have been waiting a long time for your arrival. You are on your way to free our land, and we have been praying for you. Warrior monk, you have done well, bringing them safely thus far."

The woman's eyes were dark, and Rapunzel felt as though she had met her before. But how could that be possible?

The woman smiled and stepped toward Rapunzel, reaching for her hands. Rapunzel allowed her to grasp them, bewildered by the sense of familiarity. "Princess, you have traveled a long way, and still have a ways to go. But first, our Savior has a task for you. A song was sung over you long ago, a song you knew to be evil."

Rapunzel nodded, memories returning of the witch singing a horrible song during her isolation. Strains of the tune filled her mind, almost audible in the stillness.

"We, each of us, have lost our way at times, but the song of our Savior draws us back. Did he not call to you when you were sliding down that mountain?"

Rapunzel knew better to question how the woman knew so much of her. God was at work here. "He did—Jesu held out his hand to me."

"Indeed, he broke the bonds of darkness in your life and rewrote the song of your heart. He has blessed you with a child, a child once used for evil. You must sing over her a new song before this day is over, or the darkness will continue to spread. Bless her with your love and teach her of your Savior."

"Of course I will teach her, but how do I know the words to a new song? I am not a troubadour or jester."

Amis handed the reins of the horses to Dietz and came to stand beside her. "You don't have to be a prophetic fool to know the truth of what God has placed in your heart. Sing over your daughter so that she will learn and never forget."

Rapunzel began to hum a variation of the twisted tune that the witch had sung over her. As she hummed, words came to her, the melody transforming into something new like a butterfly freed of its cocoon.

Deep in the mountain you were held,
I did not know of your life.
Deep in the mountain we did go,
And we fought Ute in our strife.
But Jesu called to me
And I surrendered there
And he freed us from her grasp
Deep in the mountain we were freed
Let this story be your seed.

Accept his peace, it is yours, my child,
As long as you keep the truth.
Accept his life, for you he died
As long as you keep the truth.

Oh, child, remember the truth!
For this truth shall set you free.
Please, child, only cling to the truth!
This is all you need from me.

The Dark Wood was shot through with light at the singing of the song. The woman lifted her hands in worship, and light shone all about her, her voice sounding like a harp as she spoke. "Come into our home that we might minister to your needs. You have a long ways yet to go."

THE CHOICE

He couldn't sleep again. A smell like onions and garlic hung in the air tonight, as though someone was breathing it out as they slept. Edmund rolled over again, careful not to shake his bunk.

It wasn't working. Nothing was working. He couldn't be what he was supposed to be, and now he couldn't even sleep. The prince took a deep breath and then nearly coughed as the stench clouded his senses. He had to get out, he needed to breathe again.

Being the heir to the kingdom had a few privileges, such as choosing the bottom bunk. He was able to slip out easily and made his way to the upper deck where Hazm and other sailors were quietly keeping the ship moving forward, checking sails, staying on course. The old sailor smiled and nodded to Edmund before he finished coiling some rope he had been working with. The moon kept her vigil high in the sky, her light spilling over and lighting the sea below. There glimmered a path through the waters. Why couldn't his path in life be so well defined?

Out on the farthest tip of the path of light there was a

dot of darkness. Of course there was. His life was defined by such darkness. For just the space of a moment, when he had escaped the baker, he had imagined himself safe. He had thought that his life could be something more, that he could use his life for the good of others. Now he was to be king, but what would he be bringing with him to the throne?

As her head came into view, he was unsurprised. It only made sense that she was waiting for him. Oddly, her leviathan face transformed into that of a woman as she approached. He had seen this face before, and he found it even more unsettling than her leviathan form. Draped once more in a shimmering garment, she climbed aboard the ship. A glance over his shoulder revealed Hazm and the others, comatose once more. They really should rethink who they put on night watch duty.

"My prince?" Her voice was rough, gritty like sand.

"What do you want?"

Her laughter rose as though from beneath the waves, as though it had been waiting to surface. "I like that you're a bit tired of me. That's as it should be."

"What do you want?" he repeated, his tone flat. They had done this before. All of this had happened before, and he was worn through. He couldn't change things, he couldn't make things right—the idea of starting over was a dream from which he was waking. He found it as elusive as the sleep that evaded him night after night.

"What does your father want of you?" She towered over him even in her human form. She was tall as a horse and more frightening than he cared to admit.

Or was she?

"You can't do anything without me, can you?"

Her head leaned to the side, her eyes sliding over his form. "Explain."

"You keep close to me and follow me around, hoping to

obtain more power, but if I never make another wish, what will happen? Will you wither and fade? And what if I discovered a way to take back my wishes? What if—"

"You can't, you foolish prince. It doesn't work that way."

He refused to let go. "But I can deny you. I can stop wishing. And I haven't made another wish since last winter."

He hated how her pale eyes lingered over him, measuring, just like his father measured. But it seemed she found something to her liking. She leaned close to his face, her breath smelling of rotten seafood. "I think you will."

"I will what?"

"Wish again."

"There's no reason that I should. There's nothing you can give me that would make it worthwhile for me."

"To the best of your knowledge. But you know very well that you know very little."

He couldn't answer her as he watched her finger extend over the bow of the ship. The darkness had grown closer and was clearly now in the shape of a ship. The flag blowing in the wind above the black sails gave him pause.

Camilla leaned in again and kissed him on his cheek before he jerked back. "A gift for you, my prince." And then she was gone, leaving Edmund to look about him in a sleep-deprived stupor. Was he seeing things? Had he imagined—?

But Hazm jerked himself awake. "Your Highness? Couldn't sleep ag—" But the old sailor froze for a moment's time as his wrinkled eyes widened. The sailor became a blur of motion. "Pirates! Pirates are heading this way!" he bellowed.

"What can I do?" Edmund sputtered, but Hazm was gone, waking the captain, rousing the rest of the crew. Without knowing what else to do, Edmund returned belowdecks, waking Georgius with his brother. "Pirates!"

The men were up and stumbling over one another to get

their clothes on, their weapons in hand. By the time they emerged, the sailors had adjusted the sails to try to outrun the advancing ship, but Edmund could see it was no use. He watched in horror as the ship sped toward them, unnaturally defying the laws of the wind and the sea as Camilla propelled it forward. While he had thought their ship was huge, it was dwarfed by the monstrosity that sidled up next to them. Screams and shouts filled the early morning air as the other crew grasped long ropes and swung across onto the deck of their ship. The metallic clang of swords unsheathing, clashing into other swords, was jarring. Was this really happening? He shook his head. Now was not the time to question or think. Now was the time to act!

Screaming as they streamed across from one ship to another, the pirates seemed more like banshees, dark-skinned women intent on harm. Edmund knew better than to underestimate them, but he saw that others did not recognize the danger as they should. Hazm was the first to fall at the blade of a woman, her sword thrust through him so neatly, it was apparent she had done this before.

Edmund stepped forward, his blade raised to strike. Even though he had seen with his own eyes her efficiency, her strength jarred him, pain radiating up his arm. There was no more time to register each strike. He stepped back and back as she attacked. He tried to recall the footwork the brothers had taught him, but he could feel himself panicking as she came closer. He narrowly pushed her back as she tried to strike a killing blow. She hissed at him, the whites of her eyes glowing in contrast to her dark lashes. But suddenly she gasped and dropped forward to one knee. Gwynndolen stood behind her, her red braid flipped over a shoulder as she spun around and slashed the woman's head from her body. Edmund looked away as the head thumped and rolled away.

There was no time to congratulate Gwynndolen, even if

killing someone was something you should congratulate a lady about. The pirates turned as one to recognize one of their own had fallen. They roared in response, their frenzied fighting taking on a barbaric tone.

"Come!" shouted Gwynndolen, and like when they had trained before, he found himself back-to-back with her, their blades pointed out as they fended off the enemy.

The women were crying out in some foreign language, one he had heard while at the Ports, and Camilla rose from the waters again, her monstrous form humongous. She swirled around the ships, the cacophony of the fighting and the breaking waves washing over Edmund like a pandemonium from which he might never wake. People were falling, struck down, the deck littered with the dead and dying.

"Protect the king and the queen!" Georgius called out as he ran forward to try to stop a would-be assassin from going below. Not quickly enough. A large woman emerged from the doorway, a knife held to the throat of the king. "Drop your swords!" she cried. "Or we kill the nobles!" Another woman came out, holding a knife to his mother's throat.

"We drop our swords when you leave!" This heated reply came from Gwynndolen as she used her short stature to advantage, tripping the assailant and thrusting a sword through her midsection. The woman coughed up blood before dropping to the deck. The deck was now littered with bodies, a mix of pirates and their compatriots on the voyage.

But a pirate came up behind Gwynndolen's back, now exposed. She snatched the long red braid back, slipping a knife beneath Gwynndolen's chin. "Do it!" came the booming, sharp voice of the pirate still holding the king.

"No!" screamed Edmund, and he struck against the woman, whose hand slipped, slitting Gwynndolen's throat. Edmund uttered a primal scream, making his voice heard above the sound of the hull cracking as the two ships met: "I wish for her to live, bring back Gwynndolen!" He quaked at the sound of his own voice, shuddering to find himself shrouded in darkness, his heart wrapped in fear, facing the human form of Camilla, whose pale eyes mocked him. "Thank you!"

It felt like shards of glass were being ground into his joints. Camilla grew, her form shifting back into a leviathan, her eyes unchanging in their evil stare.

"Wait! I wish to be free of you—"

"Oh, little prince, you can't wish that now. It's too late, because you've given me back my power! What you've asked for is so big, I don't think you understand. There is only one way to give you what you want, only one way to make it better." Her tail lashed out at the sea, causing the ships to break apart. Screams rose all around him as water began to fill the upper and lower decks, but Edmund only had a moment to recognize what was happening. For just then, a huge shadow covered him, along with Gwynndolen's broken form. And all became dark.

A TALE OF THREE SISTERS

*A*mis felt it as he finished filling the dishes for breaking fast and came to sit beside the fire. He felt a slight push, as though a large stone had been dropped far away in the middle of a lake. Ripples radiated outward in concentric circles from the source, pushing farther and farther. The sisters were reunited, able to connect. Was this the end or the beginning?

"What are you thinking, my wise fool?" Rapunzel had a bemused look on her face.

Should he tell them? They had become so carefree after the Sisters of the Light had taken them in; continuing the journey had felt joyous at last. Light piercing the darkness had been a gift from God. They didn't know what they were about to walk—well, ride—into. But how to tell them? He felt his face both frown and smile and he rose to bounce on his tiptoes. "I have another tale to tell."

"Oh, I'm so glad! I hoped that was the case."

Even little Helena seemed pleased, gurgling and clapping her chubby hands together.

For the little tyke, he stretched his limbs and then began

to juggle fruit, making certain to time each flip in order to catch the objects he was juggling. And then he tossed them to his friends, making certain to toss two to Paul. Rapunzel never could catch, especially not with her lap full of a happy child.

"Once, there were three sisters. They went nearly everywhere together. They had no brothers, but their father didn't seem to mind. In fact, he was quite boastful of his girls and decided to take them under his wing and guide them in his trade."

"How unusual," Katterina murmured.

"I know, My Lady, but he was quite an unusual man, and he looked beyond their gender to their potential. He saw great promise, like a king who might look at his daughter and think of her beauty and virtue as the asset that might ally a kingdom with another at the time of her betrothal."

"A woman is worth more than that," Katterina snapped, and Amis couldn't blame her.

"Oh, I know, My Lady. Women are more than pawns to be traded or even—excuse me for this—vessels to impregnate. Women are more than the sum of their parts—they were created by God because man couldn't bear to be alone. It was not good for him. Am I saying that right, Jacob?"

Jacob's firm mouth lifted slightly. "I know it to be true better than most."

Amis gave a little nod of his head and waggled his thick, dark eyebrows as he widened his bright blue eyes. "And you see, the man knew some of this. He knew that his girls were valuable, but he thought they were weapons to wield. He would make any sacrifice in order for them to reach their potential."

He let the word *sacrifice* fill the minds of his listeners. He picked up the thread of the story and proceeded. "These sisters learned their father's trade, and they could change shape at will. They learned the art of war with an ease that most practitioners would envy. But when the War of Sorcery stalled, their father realized that in order to gain more, he would have to make a sacrifice and kill the thing he loved in order to gain the thing he wanted."

Recognition dawned across the faces of his listeners. A somber silence fell, but he waited, drawing them out.

Rapunzel swayed the little one in her lap. "Why did he need to make a sacrifice?"

"Because the power he longed for was not his to take. It was unnatural, and the God of heaven did not want him to have it."

"I always wonder why God doesn't stop such things—I know that our ability to choose right or wrong is a gift, but we make such a mess of that beautiful gift . . . I would like to offer Helena a cleaner, tidier world."

Jacob spoke up. "You can offer her your hard-earned wisdom and continue to sing the truth to her—that there is a Savior who wants to free her from the nefarious passions of this world so that she can embrace the humble and teachable spirit God treasures."

Rapunzel nodded at the monk's wise words, and Amis picked up his strand of the story once more. "As you know, the grand sorcerer sacrificed his wife for the power he needed to win the War of Sorcery. The power filled his daughters; power he believed would give him control. Ute left for the Northlands and, as a dragon, she terrorized the generals and common people. Amee went to the Eastern Ports as a vicious centaur, while Camilla ravaged the ships at sea. But the sisters also linked their thoughts and spoke to one another without their father's knowledge. And without his knowing, when the sisters thought they had turned the tide of the war in their favor, they gathered to kill him." And

Amis stopped. This next part, they needed to summarize themselves.

"And they did kill him," Rapunzel whispered.

Paul took Helena. "And he cursed them."

"And for a long time we were blissfully unaware of how they had been communicating with one another and planning to rise up again," Jacob finished.

"But now we know. We know this, Amis. What is it you are trying to tell us? My sister Eufemia is dead and cannot carry messages back and forth. Ute is dead, separating them forever." But Katterina held herself; did she know how her voice betrayed her doubt?

"Not forever. They have found their own sacrifices and relinked."

"What does this mean?"

Amis could feel an unfamiliar frown pulling at his face. He hated to be serious. "Camilla can now join her sister Amee at the Eastern Ports. We need to hurry—we have people to warn."

SAVED AND LOST

Whisked into the air, suspended high above the wreckage of the ships, Edmund and Gwynndolen moved at great speed. They were cold, so very cold as the air around them goose-pimpled their flesh and left them shivering. Heads knocked together as they landed in a heap on shore. Edmund grabbed hold of Gwynndolen, bearing the pain deep in his joints, hugging the girl to his chest. He gathered his courage and lifted her head. Was she dead, or had his wish saved her? Her neck was whole beneath his fingers, not even a drop of blood. He cradled her close to him, rubbing her back, moaning into her hair. What had he done? What had Camilla done? What price for this life?

And now, though he had saved Gwynndolen, he had lost his father, his mother, and his wise friend. There would be no new beginning. There was nothing left for him, no matter what Georgius had said. Camilla was right: he could never escape.

Amee stood at the Ports in her human form as night fell, her position on the shore giving her a clear view of her sister emerging from the waters and coming closer. "Are we free?"

"We are. At last, all the sacrifices have been worth it, sister. We can do what we must to rid this world of the taint that separated us."

Amee frowned. Their father was dead; *he* was the one who had separated them, hadn't he? And what of the child she had given, and the one she was yet supposed to give? She wanted to believe that now, together already, it was enough.

"Gather your followers and we will—"

"I have. They are, even now, awaiting us in the marsh. Are your people coming?"

Camilla shot her a look that always made Amee feel foolish. "I thought Eufemia would have explained. Your part was to have covens that could dig in deep throughout the swamps and the Dark Wood. Mine was to raise a naval force. And I did."

The mischievous smirk on her sister's face begged interpretation. Camilla had always liked to elaborate. Amee nodded. "Well?"

"I don't think they were what Ute originally wanted, but, now that I think about it, they *are* covens, of a sort. I command the pirates from the Land of Midnight."

"But no one has seen the people for, what, two centuries? No one dares to go to shore." Amee thought of the displaced people of the Eastern Ports who worked alongside her. She had been surprised by what they already knew, at how they diligently practiced their arts once she had fully trained them. Together, for decades, they had been weaving it all into a weapon that would win the war and free them. There were times she was exhausted by the mere thought of what was ahead. In the secret parts of her heart, she wondered if there wasn't some way that she could just retreat to a new land. Everyone would be free to practice as they each preferred. Why so many sacrifices, why so much bloodshed behind—and still ahead?

"Do you remember where I was bound, sister?"

"The Illyan Sea."

"And mother always told us that it contained wonders. She was right—and one of them is that it grows seaweed that, when brewed with the seed of the ollio plant, an elixir is made to cure the plague. All who drink it become well, and those who have never had the plague are no longer in danger of getting it. Of course, they must continue to drink it, and for years I have helped them with that.

"You know, I like them. Though their ancestors were the ones who brought that weak god to the Ports and then into Alleria and beyond. Those who follow me have rejected that faith and adopted our magic as their own. Did you know, some of our followers escaped to the Land of Midnight after the War of Sorcery? Isolation made our magic stronger in that land, strangling out the faith of the weak god there. Once they were bound to me, they began doing as I bid them. They saw how easy it was to take advantage of nearby seafaring vessels." She let her hoarse voice suspend in the air. She was enjoying this more than Amee was.

"And?" Amee obediently prompted.

"And they began to pillage—just the boats. They didn't want to follow anyone back to shore. It was easy, so easy for them to take advantage of each vessel. They are mostly women, you know? It seems that the plague killed any man not able to withstand it. Now there are few men left. I rather find that fitting. Women to rule, to wage war. And they will have to, if they want to continue their line. They will have to find strong men who can father children."

A shudder rolled through Amee. She cared deeply for her covens. She wasn't sure that she wanted these women—these pirates—to come ashore to find husbands. But that couldn't be something she worried about now. That would be for later, after the war was finished. The Midnight women would fight out on the sea, and her covens would fight here, able to use the secrets of the swamp to their advantage.

"Take me to your people, my sister, and tell me what nonsense the High King is planning. Let us make plans for the first wave of attack."

THE WISH

Gwynndolen woke, clutched to Edmund's chest. She had to push firmly against him in order to find freedom to breathe. Staring up into his face, Gwynndolen was so startled by the grief and self-recrimination carved into the grooves of his tear-soaked frown that she was speechless.

What had happened? She tried to recall. Frantic shouts, the sharp smell of iron and salt, and piercing pain at her throat. She touched it gingerly. Nothing, not even a scratch. But hadn't she been cut? She blinked, trying to concentrate. What had happened before that moment? Pirates. Women? Shrieking, fighting, cursing, spitting—Edmund at her back, fighting alongside her. Where were her brothers? She looked around her. Nothing but sand for miles to either side of her and the aqua sea lapping up to lick the sand before returning to the—what sea was this?

Where was she? She stared into Edmund's bloodshot eyes. Where were they?

"I did it." His eyes were dilated in pain. But pain from what? What had he done?

"What?"

"I wished to save your life."

"You saved me?"

He shook his head as though he could deny the truth. He had *wished?*

"There was a fight. Pirates? Lots of blood—who died?"

"You were dying. I didn't know what else to do. I wanted to save you."

Her hands found their way back to her neck, where a slice had spilled out her life's blood. But he had saved her?

Suddenly she stood, jerked upright by a single thought. "What was the cost?"

"I'm not sure, she broke up both ships. They were sinking, after I wished you safe—"

"She?" Gwynndolen looked at him stupidly. "*She*, the sorceress, the leviathan?"

Edmund nodded. "Camilla."

"And she sent us here?"

"Yes."

"And the others?"

"I think they are dead, lost at sea."

No. Her mind wouldn't accept it. She couldn't be alive while her siblings lay dead at the bottom of the sea. And the king and the queen? "All of them, gone?"

"And now she is more powerful than—"

"She wanted you to wish."

"She did."

"And you *did?*"

He growled, "I couldn't just let you die."

"Yes, you could have. You should have. Why would you keep me alive? The kingdoms aren't safe now that she has more power!"

"The kingdoms weren't safe anyway. I couldn't let her take your life. If only she had taken mine instead."

Gwynndolen puffed out a sound of derision, part laugh, part grunt. "You're the crown prince. You can't die."

"It would be better if I did. I just made things worse. Why couldn't she let you and the others live?"

"Because now she has you. You want to know how your life matters, or doesn't matter? It matters immensely. Your kingdom needs you. We must figure a way out of this. Where are we?"

Edmund looked at her in shock. Her practicality, her intense logic defied his emotions, but she didn't care. "We can't unwish what you wished, can we? But we can move forward. Pick a direction."

"What?"

"Pick a direction!"

"East."

"Very well, is the sun rising or setting?" She pointed to her left where the sun was shooting off pinks and peaches that lit the sky.

Edmund nodded. "It is rising."

She pinched her lips together; at least there was something they could do. "So we can set off this way." And with this, she began walking, Edmund trailing behind like a beaten pup.

RAPUNZEL LOOKED around when she finished wiping off Helena's sticky hands after breaking fast. The child's appetite astounded her! She was growing bigger and heavier every day. She hoisted the child to her hip and looked around. Jacob and Paul were off to the side of the carriages talking and, for a moment, Rapunzel felt excluded. She took a deep breath. She didn't want to fall into that pit again, being jealously controlling enough to want to know every snippet of information. She would simply ask what they were deciding.

Jacob was nodding his head as she approached, his voice strong and steady: "Then I will go to the Father while you travel as quickly as you can to the king. It only makes sense."

"What only makes sense?" Rapunzel asked as she came up to them. The babe reached for Paul, and he took her. Jacob gave a small bow and went to get ready to leave.

"We have to divide our group now instead of later. Jacob will head to the monastery to tell the Father. He will try to raise a group of warrior monks to meet up with us at the High King's castle."

"Now *instead* of later?"

"What?"

"You said 'now instead of later.' Were you planning on us splitting up all along?"

Paul set Helena down as though to gather his thoughts. "Yes, my uncle wanted Jacob to go speak with the Father about our dealings with Ute."

"Why didn't you tell me?"

"I didn't see a need to worry you."

"Why should that worry me?"

Paul's jaw tensed. "I'm not saying it should. I thought it might, and I wanted to—"

"Why—why wouldn't you trust me?"

"You were overwrought with worry about Helena, and then Dorothea died, and it just didn't seem necessary to add to your burden."

"But my mother knew, didn't she?"

"What do you mean?"

"Something she said . . . How am I to be your wife—to be queen, if I don't know what is going on? Do you think I'm not capable—?"

"No, that's not it at all. There are some things that I can't always discuss with you—"

"I see." She stepped back as though struck. "I thought you wanted to rule together."

"I do. We will! You are misunderstanding me. There are some things that—"

Rapunzel held up her hands. "You understand far more about ruling than I do." She took Helena and left.

THE EASTERN PORTS

*E*dmund was tired of walking, tired of moving. His boots were not made for sand, and he was more than grateful when they arrived at the first village, inland a bit and away from the shore. "Solid ground beneath our feet," he said aloud, but the dark-skinned villagers laughed at his speech. He realized his mistake and switched to Latin so that the people could understand him. Camilla must have flung them upon the Eastern Ports.

Gwynndolen looked as though she could comprehend what he was saying, but she didn't seem interested in conversing. He inquired after their health and asked for food to eat at a mud-and-wattle alehouse, offering to pay with a song. He lifted his voice high and clear and told of dragons and monsters that tried to stop a hero but met a bloody end. The alehouse roared with laughter at all the right places and shed a few tears when the hero sacrificed himself for others. The drinking crowd dwindled afterward as Edmund and Gwynndolen supped, the host and his daughters cleaning up nearby.

"You must be careful where you step, young troubadour,

if you are to keep traveling. The Eastern Ports aren't known for solid footing." The man's brown skin glinted by the light of the huge hearth.

Edmund smiled and laughed with the proprietor when he warned of soft spots where a man could get stuck for days, if not worse. "We have dragons and monsters of our own, you know." The laughter ended abruptly over a gruesome tale involving large swamp-dwelling creatures who liked to snap the legs off of people who weren't watching closely. Edmund, from his travels as a troubadour, knew such creatures were about. Gwynndolen's eyes, though, were wide at the thought. He would have to watch out for her, though she might protest. For her benefit, he asked a question whose answer he already knew. "What do you call these monsters with wide mouths?"

The host plopped down into a chair beside the hearth, leaving the remainder of the work for the morning. "Oh, we call them crocodiles. They are kin to dragons and lizards and seem slow-moving at first. But don't be fooled, and don't sleep too close to the waters."

Edmund smiled as though he hadn't a care in the world. He was happy that his songs could buy them a meal with some bread left for morning. But his companion was icy and silent. What was wrong with Gwynndolen?

When they set off the next day, he noticed his companion's ever-watchful gaze darting about, and inquired. "Are you looking for crocodiles?"

"I don't want to lose my legs, you know." She looked up at him, her dark eyes snapping as though he was at fault for inventing the idea of crocodiles.

"And that's what's bothering you?"

"Yes—no. What exactly are we setting off to do, Your Highness? We walk all the way to the Eastern Ports and present the king with . . . what?"

Edmund frowned. He knew he needed to explain the urgency of their journey to her, but he felt as though he couldn't even grasp it himself. They needed to hurry, to get to the Ports and speak to the king to warn him, but he now had no tribute to give his sovereign except dire news of imminent danger. Oh, that he had two horses from the ship now sunk! "We will warn the king and tell him what happened."

"We tell him the sisters of sorcery have at last reunited because you made a foolish wish?" she spluttered.

"How can you be mad at me?"

She reeled around to face him. "How can I be—? How can I not be mad? My brothers—my sister—your parents—all dead! You knew she was baiting you, that she wanted you to make a wish. You shouldn't have done it. Why would you put our loved ones—the entire kingdom in danger for —for—"

"For you? Why would I put the kingdom in danger for *you*?" They stared at each other, and he tried to hold his anger in check. "Do you really want me to answer that?"

Her face was bright pink, making her freckles pop out. "Yes, fine! Why would you want to save my life at the cost of the kingdom? You can't possibly think my life is worth—"

He reached around her and pulled her into him, dipping his face low to brush his lips to hers, but she flung herself back.

"What are you doing?"

Stunned, he just stared at her, his hands foolishly outstretched.

"Are you trying to kiss me? The kingdom's in danger and I ask you for an explanation—and you're trying to *kiss* me?"

"Gwynndolen!" He covered the distance of her retreat with a single step. He'd had enough of her ire and wanted some consideration, but she stepped back again.

"What?"

"I'm not, just—just stand there. Please?"

"Why? So you can kiss me?"

"Would that be awful?"

"If people *died* for you to get to kiss me, then yes, it would be awful."

"It wasn't so that I could kiss you. I was simply trying to explain—" He halted. Should he start over? She didn't understand, but how could he make her understand? "I made a promise to myself long ago, never to let someone die if it was in my power to stop it. Someone did die, once, and I could have stopped it if I had just used my power of the wish, but I didn't. Not in time to save her."

Gwynndolen narrowed her eyes as her hands crossed tightly over her chest. "But you did save Rapunzel in time."

"It wasn't Rapunzel I let die."

THE WIND RIPPLED through the leaves overhead, creating a murmur like the sound of the waves on the shore. Jacob was tempted to relax his guard at the sound, but at once he pulled himself upright. At Paul's urging, he had selected a trusted knight to take over as company commander, and he had set off at once with Amis for the Eastern Ports. They rested only when they had need to, trading horses when they could. At this rate, the trip that would take another month for the large group with a carriage and supply wagon would be reduced to a little over a week for the men. The humidity increased, but not like at the Fisher King's shore. It was a warm humidity that hummed with the buzzing of insects and the sound of cicadas. Their bright chirruping buzz thrummed in Jacob's ears. He gazed into the branches draped with hanging tufts of grey moss. It reminded him of an old woman's grizzled hair. The urgency in his breast stalled for a moment as nostalgia filled him. This was the land of his birth, the adopted home of his people. He wondered if his mother was still alive and what had ever happened to the men who raised him in the order.

"Jacob?" Amis inquired beside him, their horses stamping the ground in impatience at the halt.

But there was no time to reminisce, he reminded himself. He jerked his head toward the road and Amis nodded. Jacob dug his heels into his obedient steed. God was with them to provide such sure-footed creatures that responded as though they had been traveling companions for far longer than a matter of days. If they hurried, perhaps they could make it tonight.

CURSED

Gwynndolen's mouth dropped, the reality of Edmund's burden sinking in. "What do you mean, you caused someone's death? Whose?"

He turned away. "It was the baker's wife, Cibell. In a way, she was like my mother. She would comfort me when Elias would force me to wish, making my bones and joints ache. He began by tempting me with treats, but as I grew older and the pain mounted, the treats weren't enough. Instead, he beat me. But what he was asking me to do—even as young as I was, I could see it was wrong. I could *feel* it, as though God himself was protesting through my very bones. When he could no longer tempt me or beat me into submission, he turned on Cibell."

He turned to look at Gwynndolen, eyes moist. "I would do anything to keep him from hurting her, even the worst things, but she begged me to stop. She knew he was horrible, that he was getting worse as his power over me grew. When she saw I wouldn't stop, that he never would, she sacrificed herself to set me free. I had tried to wish myself free from him, and her as well—but it didn't work. I was so very young, and all I knew was this life of doing what he wanted. Only after she killed herself did I finally run away. I resisted using my wish for many years, only giving in when my belly was too empty, or for the pink."

"What is the pink?"

His lips slanted into a smile beneath the scruff of mustache he had not shaved since leaving the ship. "When I was very young, I imagined and then wished for a pink little girl to play with me. Outside of Cibell, she was my only solace. She was like a rose—sweet-smelling, but she had no thorns. She would sing to me about who I was meant to be."

"She sounds like an angel sent to comfort you when you needed it most."

"But I wished her into being."

Gwynndolen thought on this. "But God allowed you to have the power of the wish. He allowed Camilla to give that to you. What if—"

"No, don't say it . . ." But he looked at her as though he now doubted whether the wish was all a curse or not. He gave a little shake of his head, as though to shrug off a gnat before continuing the tale. "I couldn't take the pink with me when I escaped the baker, so I made her into a rose."

"The one on your lute?"

"Yes—I didn't mind the pain of that wish. I could carry her with me everywhere. If only I had her now, I could get us better lodging, better food. Sometimes I think about the pink, what she might sing. What would she think of the choices I've made? She used to tell me to pray, that things would get better, that somehow God had a plan. I thought—"

Gwynndolen inclined her head and waited for him to continue.

It took him a moment, but he finally picked up his thoughts once more. "I wanted it all to mean something.

Cibell's death, my songs, my pink playmate—and then Rapunzel—I imagined she was the pink sent from heaven. But I suppose I've hurt everyone I've ever loved."

Gwynndolen tried to make sense of the turmoil that was swirling his past together into a fog of despair. "But you saved Rapunzel."

"I was selfish. I saved Rapunzel because I thought I could make her what I wanted. She reminded me of the pink and —I thought that was love. I was wrong. It was selfish, and that isn't love as it should be."

Gwynndolen contemplated as the silence between them lingered. She only broke it when she knew what to say. "You haven't hurt me."

"What?"

"You haven't hurt me. You saved me."

Edmund's dark eyes stared into her own, and his scowl softened. He reached out and took her hand, which she stared at for a moment too long. "I saved you because I love you. I see in you the woman who should be the next queen."

"But I haven't been raised to it! I'm not of noble blood. You wouldn't even know me if I hadn't been adopted. I have nothing to bring to the kingdom."

"Except your will. Except your spirit. Except your wisdom. You anchor me like no one ever has. There is nothing I can do that you will go along with unless you believe it is right. I cannot wish you into submission—you will always stand on your own."

Her shoulders lifted because this only made sense. "Of course I will."

"Don't you know how rare that is? Don't you know how I need that—how Rona needs that? I don't need a woman I can bend to my will. I also don't need a preening woman who delves into gossip at court. I just need you."

Gwynndolen looked around them, the sprawling

branches overhead full of brightly colored birds. They weren't quiet, but she had been so intent on his words that she hadn't heard their cawing. She took a deep breath and hazarded a look into his eyes. "But why sacrifice it all for—"

"I didn't think, I just knew I couldn't lose you."

"But how many have we lost because of it? Your parents, my siblings—"

His cheeks flushed and his eyes flashed, but it looked like shame, not anger. "I know that now! But at the time—I didn't know what else to do!"

Gwynndolen frowned. "You gave Camilla what she wanted. She has the power now."

"I know, which is why we must reach the High King."

"But how can we—"

He lifted a finger to her lips. "I don't know. I don't know the answers to any questions, I only know that it wasn't right to let you die. Did you know my mother made me promise to keep you safe? She had her reasons, and I think I understand them now. Camilla thinks she's won, but we mustn't let her. We will find a way."

Gwynndolen looked up at him then and raised her eyebrow. "Then we need to find a couple of horses. Do you have any tales worth a couple of horses?"

"Only if we find the right audience." He took a step forward and leaned down to brush his lips to hers. For just a moment, he lingered and she let him. She didn't kiss back, but she didn't stomp away this time, either. She blinked as he stood upright again.

"What was that for?" She could hear her tone was laced with a bit of suspicion and a hint of something else.

He shrugged his shoulders and smiled. "Let's go find a rich lord with horses."

THE MONASTERY

Amis laughed when they entered the city midmorning, sun now heating the air about them. "These poor little squatty homes!" Amis pointed at several that had not been built on a firm foundation and had sunk into the mire. Jacob nodded. Such sights were familiar in his memory, and within him nostalgia mixed with sorrow. He wished Katterina beside him instead of the laughing fool. He knew she would understand. Here he was, returning to the home of his birth, surrounded by people who looked like him, talked like him—but he was no longer one of them. He had been away too long, grown used to other customs, other languages.

Jacob and Amis found their way to the monastery slowly, having to make allowances for city dwellers traveling to and from the market on foot. He had time to make note of a few strange homes that rested on stilts, like a little boy struggling to look over the shoulder of his big brother. It was clear these were trying not to sink, but only half succeeded, there in the poorest section of the city.

As they drew nearer the monastery, the buildings became

more stable, the ground more solid, with layers of rocky gravel spread throughout the years when the nobles brought it in boatloads from the Northlands.

Monks stood on guard outside a gate, part of a wall which fenced in the monastery's grounds. Jacob was glad as they opened the well-oiled gate for them that he had kept his tonsure clean-shaven to be recognized as part of the order. The grounds leading to the temple were extensive, sprinkled with buildings where young orphans were taught how to think and live. The yards were well tended, gardens bursting with magentas and golden ochres. Fruit trees were blooming. He wondered, though the thought had never before occurred to him, how much time it had taken for the slaves to raise the ground and put in drains. He knew little of the people who had curated the land long ago before slavery had been outlawed. But before he could dwell long on this, the temple came into view.

The monastery was not as large as he remembered from his youth, but was still imposing with its marble columns and grandiose stained-glass windows. It sat staring out as though daring only those worthy to enter. Jacob and Amis dismounted and approached the monks who stood watch. One tall man stared down at Jacob from his lofty height. "I'm here to see the Father. My name is Brother Jacob, and I was guided by the Father in my youth when he was still only Brother Iohannes. I now hail from the Fisher King's realm in the Northlands. My companion is Amis the fool, a prophet also sent by our king. We have urgent news, if you please."

The man's face remained stone. "Wait here," he said in a distant tone, leaving the other watchman to guard the entrance while he made his way inside.

Jacob stood up straight and tall, knowing that his North-land garb had told the guards at first sight that he was no longer one of them. For a brief moment he wondered, if he were told to return here to serve close to what had been his home, would he be able to acclimate once more? He wasn't sure he could, and he didn't want to try. He hoped that nothing would change his plans of returning to the North-lands, the place that had become more a home to him than what he had ever experienced in the land of his birth.

Living among people he did not look or sound like had eventually become normal for Jacob, but he hadn't realized till now how much he had grown used to the Northlanders' ways. Did the warrior monk look or sound like other North-landers? No—he had become something in between. *Is this what my ancestors from the Land of Midnight felt when they traveled back and forth between the Eastern Ports and the Land of Midnight?* he wondered. Now no one could return to that point of origin and share what he was now experiencing—how they had become *other*, a new people no longer the same as the old. Not unless the plagues had ceased, and how would they find that out?

The man returned, cutting off Jacob's musings. He looked at Jacob and Amis with veiled curiosity. "The Father has just come from *terce* and looks forward to meeting with you." The guard led them through the halls, and Amis openly admired the beautiful icons in the hallways.

"What's terce?" Amis piped up as he followed.

"Midmorning prayers."

Jacob wished they had arrived at the halls earlier so that they could hear the voices raised in prayer. He remembered how worship echoed throughout the halls, recalled the beauty of the men's harmony and the beat of their fighting staffs on the ground. They would chant and sing in worship, bringing order and rhythm in their methodically timed prayers. No one need look at the sun at the monastery to discover the time of day; all one had to do was open his ears and hear what prayers of song were filling the air.

Jacob had missed that. The absence of prayers and their corporate rhythms had been disconcerting when he, as a young man, discovered he was not to return from the Northlands. Serving alongside the then-Fisher Prince was an adjustment. There were no other monks to keep prayer with him. The monk who had served there before him had become ill and needed to return to the Eastern Ports for his health, but he had died and never returned. There had been no replacement, and Jacob was forced to find a different kind of rhythm to his day. Though he prayed regularly, he did not meet with others to do so. There was no chanting or singing or beating out the rhythm on the ground with his fighting staff. Daily exercise was done with knights. He laughed inwardly, remembering his first awkward interactions with them. *They* did not time their strikes with scripture. He had taught some of these things to the Fisher Prince and then to Paul, but it was not the same as what he had learned here. Such things could not be properly conducted by a single brother at a foreign outpost.

Though the absence of that fellowship and order had at first grieved him, he found a different freedom awaiting him in the Northlands. The freedom to pray at any time of day had felt strange, wrong at first. But with the freedom came a quiet joy that seeped in slowly as it revealed itself to him. He had tried to put it into words once, but the warrior in him couldn't capture the longing in his soul. What if one could have both: the freedom to worship with the strength of the fellowship as one did so? His broad lips nearly smiled as he followed the brother that led him to the nave. Ah! He felt as though the Spirit had whispered this truth to him. He was missing the Fisher King and Paul. In their friendship he had found that strength of fellowship, though different than he had known here. He looked to his right at Amis who still gawked at all around him. Yes, this fool also aided him in worshipping the one true God, though his ways were certainly unorthodox.

In the middle of the nave stood the man he'd been looking for. Father Iohannes's hair was silver around his brown tonsure. He was draped in beautiful robes embroidered with gold crosses. Such robes revealed the height of his status in the order. Though his reception was quiet, Jacob could see the joy in the man's dark eyes. "Brother Jacob, you have returned to us at long last. I am glad of your coming— it has been many years since I last saw your face."

"I trust my yearly letters have kept you apprised."

"Yes, indeed, I have looked forward each year to reading your letters, explaining how things were progressing."

"I know it is unusual that I should come myself with my message this year, but when you have heard—" Amis put a hand on Jacob's arm. The fool was no longer smiling.

"Yes, when you sent word that this year you would bring the message yourself, we were surprised, but have eagerly anticipated your return. We had been given to understand there would be a party with you, but I am told you traveled only with—?" He gestured to Amis, clearly mystified at what a fool was doing with a warrior monk. "I hope the rest of your party is safe, and something untoward hasn't happened?"

Jacob frowned slightly, but tried to begin again despite Amis's subtle shake of his jester's cap. "Something most surprising has happened on the way, and I will beg your help at the end of my tale. Trust for now that the party I traveled with was well when we left them behind, but it became urgent that we travel ahead."

"I see," stated the older monk, though the crease between his brows belied the fact. "And why would you bring with you a fool? I believe you insisted he come to meet with me as well?"

Jacob bowed his head in deference. "Yes, Father, and I thank you for trusting me in allowing him to come along with us. We have much to tell you and ask of you."

Amis was now looking at the Father as though he were a strange sort of animal, but the Father seemed unaware. Jacob tried to ignore the fool. The Father's serene face smiled and he turned his body so that he could lead them to an alcove next to hundreds of wavering candles lit for the purpose of prayer. There were two benches facing one another, Father Iohannes took a seat on one while motioning his guests to the opposite. Once seated, he opened his hands. "I would be most pleased if you would begin your tale."

Jacob opened his mouth to begin, but Amis began to laugh.

Not surprisingly, the Father looked shocked, serenity misplaced at once. "What do you mean by laughing?"

"It's only that this is all so funny," Amis stated, wiping at his eyes. "I mean, of course, it isn't funny at all, but it's so ironic, don't you think, dear brother?"

The Father almost sputtered, but held back. "I really can't say because I don't know what you are talking about."

"That's not unusual in the least. Most of the time when I begin talking, people are unsure of what I'm about. But never mind that. For the Father's sake, I will explain."

The man puffed, "I would that you would do so in haste."

Amis drew his brows together and lowered his voice dramatically. "But haste is not something that will serve our purposes at this time." Jacob couldn't understand what the fool was saying in that mocking way. "In fact, wouldn't you say, Jacob, that haste is not something that Father Iohannes is known for?"

Jacob stared at Amis for a moment and then looked

closer at the Father before answering. "No, he is most assuredly a man who takes his time."

"Any would grow weary at this lengthy preamble before hearing what was called 'urgent'—please, get to the point."

Jacob looked back at Amis, no longer sure of himself or his surroundings. He reached over to where he had placed his staff when he sat down and firmly gripped it in one hand. Were the candles truly wavering, or were they shimmering with magic? "You don't think he is who he says he is?"

Amis shook his head, mirth still causing his shining eyes to twinkle as he raised and lowered his brows. "Not only is he not who he says he is, but we aren't where we are supposed to be. Are we, mistress?"

Father Iohannes's form elongated into that of someone tall, and then stretched further, the body doubling over as though to crawl. Arms reached down, hands curling into fists that became hooves that stomped. Out of the torso a woman's body stretched up, covered with the fine hair of a horse. The facial features softened into those of a pale woman, eyes turning black and huge, lips a firm line of displeasure. Her gaze looked from Amis to Jacob as the shimmering candles dimmed and the walls of the monastery seemed to melt into the trees of the marshland. Amis was now sitting on the damp stump of a tree. Jacob had leapt up in front of him with his staff at the ready. All around, as far as the eye could see, there was moss and bog. Emerging from the waters were dark people, glistening, water dripping down their bodies.

"Where are we?" Jacob could hear it now, how his voice wasn't resonating in the halls of his youth. He should have known something was wrong when the sounds and smells of the monastery hadn't matched the memories.

"You are in my marsh. You are not going to warn anyone of anything." Her eyes never left his face. She didn't blink as she stared and stared. From the waters behind her rose the head of a leviathan that changed into that of a sneering woman. She stepped onto the soft bank and reached out a tentacle to swipe at his staff, wrapping another around him and still another around Amis. She stood calmly beside her centaur sister, looking human except for the long tentacles twisting from beneath her shimmering gown. She hissed a laugh, revealing a forked tongue. The sisters of sorcery stood before him, and what could he do? Nothing.

Amis joined her laughter.

"Why are you laughing, little man?" the leviathan asked.

Jacob understood at last, and he shifted within her grasp. "Because neither of you can see what is coming. You think you can stop God from having his way? He won't be undone by this little act."

The leviathan gripped tighter as she stepped close enough that Jacob couldn't escape her fish-breath in his face. "You think this a small thing we have done?"

"I think it a desperate thing. A thing of which you cannot understand the ramifications."

The centaur woman—Amee, he supposed—shuddered, and her hooves stamped the ground as she retreated backward. "Calm yourself, sister," Camilla commanded, her rough voice filling the air with authority. "We are the ones in control here. These two will find that we have stopped them from sharing their warning."

The centaur nodded her head a bit. "The High King, the true fool, has no idea we are awake. He seems to think we've been sleeping all this while, thinks he has nothing to worry over."

"He is wrong," the fool stated. "But he is not the one with power to do much. What needs doing will happen. We know that the God of heaven will not be stopped by you or your followers."

"What do you know of our followers?" Camilla asked with a mocking smile.

"You weave a good web, but we have met your kind before. It was we who met your sister Ute not so long ago, deep within the Soontrisse Mountains. She was defeated by the God we serve, as you will be!" Though the words were bravely spoken, Jacob could hear how weak his voice sounded as she tightened her grip. "We have met some of your followers in the Dark Wood—we know many live here, and others are coming to meet them to begin the war again."

The tentacles yanked the men off their feet and dangled them upside down. "Oh, no, foolish little men! Not to begin the war again—to finish the war. The war never stopped for us, and we will not be thrown off again!"

As the blood filled Jacob's head, he tried to concentrate on what was true. Whether he perished or not, the Savior of the world was at work, and he would be certain to make all things new, to set all things right.

"Even if you kill us, you will not win," Amis strained as she squeezed the last bit of air out of him.

"Was this something you could see, my prophetic fool?" Her laugh was hideous as her forked grey tongue flicked in and out. She loosened her hold, and they slipped and fell on their heads, splashing and spluttering in the bog.

"Well," Amis said, after gasping for air and coughing, "I knew something would happen."

Jacob tried to lunge for his staff, but in his dizziness, he stumbled. His hands were whisked behind him to be tied up by the followers of sorcery. He looked at the fool. Had he really known what was to happen? "You knew something would happen, and yet you said nothing?" he grunted.

Amis was likewise being tied up. "I said I must come with you. For alone, you would not survive." Jacob shot him a glance.

"Take them away!" Camilla directed the followers, but they looked to the centaur before obeying.

"You're saying I would die without you?" Jacob whispered as they were led away.

Amis actually grinned. "You would at that, my friend. But no worries—we are stronger together, and will soon be even stronger."

"Why is that?"

Those great, wild eyebrows raised again. "You shall see, warrior monk!"

AN UNKNOWN CASTLE

Gwynndolen felt the waves toss the ship back and forth. She hit her head as she tried to walk forward, bumping into the doorway. Shaking it off, she began to descend. She had to get to the horses in time. There had to be something she could do for them. Upon reaching their level, she blanched as she saw the ship was already taking on water. Beatrix and Georgius were there, trying to calm and steady the steeds, as though they were unaware of the water that was seeping into the boots on their feet. Gwynndolen stared hard at her brother and sister. Why would they be working together to care for the horses? Beatrix turned and looked at Gwynndolen. "It's your fault. It's your fault I'm dead. I'll never get to the High King's court or find a husband. I wasn't going to be a bother to you for much longer. Why did you get to live so that I would die?"

Georgius began to laugh, but it didn't sound like him. The laughter was cruel, twisted in a way that Gwynndolen knew couldn't be coming from her beloved brother. "Gwynndolen gets to live because the prince loves her. Her life is more valuable because she will one day be queen!"

Beatrix joined in the laughter, and this was a sound that Gwynndolen *did* recognize. "Gwynndolen, smelling of horses and manure, presented by the prince to the High King instead of me? Surely not! He's just using her to get what he wants. Maybe her earthiness grounds him, but he'll get tired of the muck and find someone like me to help him rule Rona."

The waters were churning and the horses were wide-eyed, their ears flicking back and forth. Gwynndolen stepped forward, longing to calm them, though she knew this was wrong, this was false. But when her hand reached forward, it didn't touch the side of a heaving horse, but a damp fabric of some kind.

Gwynndolen jerked awake and looked around her, pulling her blanket to her chest—but it was stuck! In the night, she had twisted and thrashed to such a degree that her blanket was wrapped around her while her chemise clung to her in a sweaty mess.

A shard of truth cut through her confusion. Dead. Everyone but Edmund was dead. For a moment she couldn't breathe. But she had to be strong, she had to keep herself together. She couldn't fall apart now, not ever. Blinking, she tried to make sense of reality.

Where was she? A dim, grey light coming in from a high window allowed her to see that she was in some sort of room. Wasn't this her bed? No. It was narrow like hers, but instead of the curtains she expected to see hanging from the bed's canopy, there was a drapery of netting. She pulled back the mesh and straightened her clothing enough to be able to stand upright. Buzzing beside her ear preceded a prickle on her skin. She swatted, but there was soon another buzz to fend off. Perhaps this was what the sailors had tried to warn her of—the insects who loved the Eastern Ports? They must be sailing close—but no, they weren't on the ship any longer.

That dream had been pieces of things her mind couldn't quite accept. The ship had sunk. Her brothers and her sister were gone.

Edmund. He was all she had left. They had been stranded by the seashore, then had made their way to a village, had started traveling on from there . . . She looked around her, feeling quite stupid. Why couldn't she remember how she came to be here?

Her feet were bare and she padded to the door, noticing that the floor was made of wood sanded smooth beneath her feet. There were no bristling rushes or hay covering it, but her feet felt gritty. Was there sand or dirt on the floor? Where were her shoes?

A curious thing. As she approached what she had thought was a doorway, she discovered no door, simply an archway leading into a hall. Why was she here? Where *was* "here"?

A sound. She held her breath. In the dim light she saw a shadow advancing and heard someone moving closer to her in the hallway.

"Gwynndolen?" Edmund's voice was low, and she was so grateful to hear it, she wanted to hug him. Instead, she reached for his arm to make certain he was solid. He was— he wasn't a dream.

"Where are we?"

"I don't know."

"What do you mean?" She asked this, though she had a growing suspicion that he was experiencing the same lapse of memory that she was.

"I was dreaming, something horrible—I don't remember what. The shape of it escapes me, but when I awoke, I was here."

"But where is *here*?"

An unsettling sound reached them, a moaning that Gwynndolen hoped was simply the sound of the structure settling. A pale light was seeping in from high windows. Not much of it, but enough for her to see that the sound disturbed Edmund as much as it disturbed her.

"You wait here and I'll—"

"I'm not waiting behind. We go together." She wanted to slip her hand into his, but that was foolish. They needed their hands free in case they needed to defend themselves.

As they moved forward down the hall, she felt naked, exposed. Was someone watching them? Someone who could see their every move and understand their every thought? Her heart beat erratically as she tried to quell the paranoid thoughts.

Next they came to a landing. The hallway opened onto a balcony that presented an open staircase leading both up and down. They choose to make their way down, Edmund in front, Gwynndolen following behind, her astute eyes measuring the subtle hints of grey becoming colors as the morning light grew brighter. Her eyes darted back and forth. When they reached the bottom of the stairs, Edmund tried to shield her with his body as he moved forward, but she pushed in front.

If only she had a weapon!

They had descended into the dwelling's Great Hall. Long, vertical windows were now filtering in shafts of light, displaying a massive table with chairs on a raised platform at the far end of the room. The table had candelabras. Gwynndolen furtively made her way to the table and snatched one for herself and another for Edmund, discarding the candles on the table.

"What are these for?" Edmund asked as she hopped down from the platform to him.

"These will make do for a weapon—unless you have a better idea, Your Highness."

Edmund nodded vaguely while looking at her with a

strange respect. "I'm sorry, I should think of such things myself."

"Well, perhaps that's why I am with you. To protect you."

Edmund laughed. "I really hope not."

A lock of hair tried to block her eyesight, but she blew it out of the way while angling her body to see the room in front of the platform, keeping her back protected by the wall behind her. "But it might be the case."

A door at the far right opened, and Gwynndolen faced it, candelabra raised.

"Ah! I see the guests are awake and up!" The voice boomed, his Latin words resounding across the hall. A gigantic man came forward dressed in finery. Servants entered behind him, filling the room with the aroma of baked bread and sweet-smelling spices. He clapped his huge hands together. "Come! We have no need for candles at this time of day, or were you thinking of swiping my head off with those things?" But he didn't allow time for them to answer. "Join me at my table and let's eat together! We can discuss all—"

"Who are you?" Gwynndolen stood her ground.

He gestured to the platform and proceeded to make his way there as he spoke. "I see you do have questions. Completely understandable. Let's just sit down and—"

"I don't sit and dine with people I don't know! Who are you?"

The man turned to Edmund. "Feisty, isn't she?"

"Gwynndolen—" Edmund said, reaching for her as though to placate her.

Gwynndolen glared at him and then the man. "Who are you, and where are we? What's wrong with our memories? Why don't we remember coming here?"

The great man laughed, his broad chest lending air that

made him louder than Gwynndolen would have thought possible.

"What's so funny? What am I not understanding?"

"Haven't you come to the Eastern Ports to meet the High King?"

Gwynndolen did not relax her stance, but Edmund answered, having already lowered his candelabra. "We are on our way to his court, yes."

"Good, then I can help you with that."

With his firm, diplomatic voice, Edmund asked, "Who are you, and why would you wish to help us?" He kept his candelabra lowered, but didn't sound at ease, which, ironically, made Gwynndolen feel more at ease.

But the man didn't answer, and a woman stepped in front of him. Her eyes were strange, black as any Ronan's but with no whites to show. She seemed to smell the air and then she blinked, every movement slow, methodical. She was there, shimmering—and then she wasn't. Was it a trick of the eye? Gwynndolen looked at Edmund. Had he seen the apparition, too?

Her look of bewilderment must have caught that of the man, because another chortle burst forth. "Ah, my child, you have seen such things as to make you wonder. Am I right? But you'll not know more until you sit with me and eat your fill."

"It is unwise—"

"Ah yes, I believe the phrase is something like, 'Hold a knife to your throat if ye be a man of great appetite when dining with an unscrupulous leader.'"

"So, you are unscrupulous?"

"You don't know if I am or I'm not. Nor do I wish you to die of hunger while under my roof. What if we tried things this way? I'm going to go sit down and allow my servants to get one large plate ready with some treats. I will take a bite of each dish. When you are satisfied that I haven't been poisoned, you can come eat."

Edmund nodded, "This seems reasonable to me." But he looked at Gwynndolen rather than the man.

Gwynndolen gave a cautious nod as well, keeping the candelabra in hand. If it came to it, the man was so big that she'd be better off trying to run instead of hitting him. Then again, there were tales of great giants that crossed great distances faster than a man could blink. Her grip tightened around the brass.

The man's actions were surprisingly dainty as he spooned some exotic fruit onto a dish and then tore off small pinches from the loaf of bread. Well—they were small pinches compared to his massive size, but huge chunks compared to Gwynndolen's mouth. He chewed, smiling all the while, then took another bite of each and smiled again.

Gwynndolen took a moment and surveyed the room more closely. The skin of the servants was far darker than that of the sailors who had served aboard the ship. As dark as the pirates—! The candelabra bit into her palm, but she didn't loosen her grip. They seemed calm, intent on caring for the host, who was just as dark. Not just deeply tanned— their skin seemed as dark as the rich soil of Rona. Their hair was coarsely textured, though the women wore it braided and partially covered near the crown, while the men's hair was cropped close to the skull and left uncovered. Their clothing was similar in style to her own, though it was clearly made of a thinner material. The lord himself was wearing a tunic of shining bright yellow silk and brown leather leggings.

A flash caught her eye, the apparition of that white shimmering woman again, her black eyes staring. She was standing beside the man, staring at his face as he chewed, but then she turned her head and looked directly at Gwynndolen. "Can you see me?" She spoke in a startled voice that sounded more vulnerable than Gwynndolen would have imagined. "I can," she replied dumbly and then frowned when the apparition faded again.

The great man laughed, almost choking on his bite. He coughed and covered his mouth, barely recovering from his outburst. "It's so strange to have someone else who can see her. I thought for a long time that it was me, my own night-mares come to life. But you see her, too." He nodded to himself and a furrow between his brows released. "You *are* the ones I'm supposed to help."

Gwynndolen glanced away from Edmund's questioning look. She wondered how long they needed to wait before they knew it was safe for them to join in eating. Her stomach gurgled and the man laughed again. "Please"—he gestured with one hand—"I mean you no harm. You can safely eat and enjoy my hospitality. I want to share how you came to be here and how I wish to help you on your way."

Gwynndolen cautiously sat down as a servant took food from the giant's plate and divided it between her and Edmund. She was unused to eating after someone, but she had to face the strange reality of their situation. Her teeth sank into the bread, and she found it surprisingly light and buttery. "Mmm." She hadn't meant the sound to escape her, but it had. Edmund grinned and took a spoonful of the cooked fruit and also let out a contented sigh, giving the giant another reason to chuckle.

"My title is simple: Lord Jalid. My family has long lived here, content to be in this part of the world, having migrated from the Land of Midnight before the plagues. You would think the land that surrounds us is too swampy to be much good, but we grow rice in rich fields. Earlier this week, after visiting the fields of my serfs, I was in the marsh heading home, and I came upon the strangest sight. The two of you were wondering around, clearly unsure of yourselves. 'How long have you been traveling?' I asked, but you struggled to answer. I could tell you were dehydrated, so I had my servants bring you back here for some nourishment, and they put you to bed."

"And what happened to our clothes?" Gwynndolen was all too aware that she was only wearing her damp chemise.

"They are heavy for the weather here, but they have been washed. You can have them back, but I'm happy to provide you with something more suitable."

A glimmer to her right caused Gwynndolen to jerk again, and then the giant laughed when Edmund frowned at her. Leaning toward Edmund, a curious gleam in his eye, the lord addressed the prince: "You can't see her, can you, Your Highness?"

ARE YOU WILLING TO SACRIFICE?

mee stopped spying, realizing she couldn't continue to do so without being spotted. She paced back and forth through the trees, wishing she could see the future instead of being able to spy on people. She thought about her family's abilities. Camilla was able to reach into the minds of people. Her father—and Ute, too, before the curse—could travel great distances to do things. But Amee had never been that strong. Still, they had all been defeated because they had underestimated those they thought were allies. What if they had seen beyond their moment of greed? What if they had been able to recognize a different outcome?

Amee lifted her hands to her face and breathed in deeply, the scent of the marsh all around her. She loved the drifting smell of dank humidity, growing moss, the salty tang that warmed the air now that spring was truly here. Soon it would be summer, and the sun would warm the waters. All would be teeming with young life. Something in her twitched. Would she be able to do what she was supposed to do? What if it meant destroying this place, her home for so many years? What if it meant hurting the people who had grown to trust her, the girl who called her mother—what if they discovered what the first sacrifice had been?

"Sister?" Camilla's voice was like sand rubbing against her senses as she approached.

"What?"

Camilla's eyes narrowed. "What are you thinking?"

"That I'm not sure what we are doing."

"What do you mean?"

She turned her thoughts toward more practical matters. Perhaps she could reason with Camilla. "Why have we bothered to capture those two men? They aren't that special. They are more trouble than they are worth, especially the one who keeps singing ridiculous songs and asking for food."

"Then use your power and make them be quiet."

Amee looked down, but her sister put a finger beneath her chin and forced her to meet her eyes. "We are finishing what Ute began. We are doing what our father should have done. We will not be distracted by mere men who would see us burned if given the chance."

Amee swallowed the retort burning in the back of her throat. "I know you're right, but—"

"You don't want to hurt your daughter."

"Not another another child. There have been too many. I am tired of the sacrifices required to fuel our sorcery."

"But without the sacrifices—"

"It's not my sacrifice or your sacrifice, it is the sacrifice of innocents who have no choice. It's like killing Mother all over again, just so that we will have more power. How can we do anything like that ever—"

"We didn't do it!" Camilla's voice thundered.

"*We* were why our father killed her."

"No, he did it because he wanted to win the war. He

killed his wife so that he could harness the power of his daughters. It was wrong."

"And it was wrong that I sacrificed my eldest." The tears that coursed down Amee's face were angry tears of rage and pain. Her face contorted in agony. "Why? Why should another die so that I could have more, so that you could have more? It was wrong!"

"No, it was the only way to make things right. None of us were to ever marry. You knew this, and still you found yourself a man. He was to serve you, not become your mate. Your children could never be more than a sacrifice—unless, of course, you had sacrificed your husband for them. Didn't matter in the end, did it? He still died, as mortals do. They are so weak."

"No! He lived a good life at my side, as both my children should be allowed to do. It's not right, what we did. What we are doing. All for power."

"No, it is for freedom! How can you not understand this still?"

"I've never understood it! I'll never understand it! I won't sacrifice another child for this, not ever again."

"Oh, sister, you don't have a choice. We began on this path and we must see it through. If you don't sacrifice your daughter, then you must sacrifice—"

"No, I will find another way! There must be another way!"

"Not if we want to be free. Don't you think that Ute looked for another way? Don't you think I did? All these years, and this blood is the only way to freedom. Go run till you can't cry anymore. Cry and run all day. Cry yourself to sleep if you must! But wake up in the morning with the resolve to slay our enemies and mingle their blood with our most precious love. Then, and only then, will we have the strength to fight this war and win. I want to be free. I want my followers to be free. Don't you?"

Amee's tear-filled eyes could just make out the blurry form of her sister. She felt weak and defeated; there was nothing she would ever be able to do. For if she sacrificed what she loved and held most dear, there would be nothing worth fighting for.

THE COUNSEL OF A DAUGHTER

Katterina sat still, staring into the darkness as the fire dwindled. Her ears picked up the sound of someone moving, but she didn't turn her head to see who it was. She already knew.

"Are you worried?" Rapunzel's whisper seemed unnecessary. Everyone was asleep around a few of the fires, except for two knights who were on watch and walking around.

"Why would I be worried?" Katterina felt her voice made more sense—lowered, but not hissing in that whispered way of her daughter.

"Mother, look at me. You can see me, can't you?"

Katterina smiled, though she knew that Rapunzel could barely see anything beneath the covering of the thick leaves they were resting under. "Yes, I can see you quite clearly."

"I thought so. You always seem to get around just fine, and the carriage darkness doesn't seem to bother you a bit."

Katterina shrugged and then laughed quietly, knowing the shrug was pointless. "Now, what is bothering you so much?"

"You—you seem so downcast since Jacob left."

Katterina tugged on a thread that was fraying on her cloak. "Yes?"

"Do you—do you want to talk about it?"

Katterina thought about how often she had tried to get Rapunzel to confide in her on their journey to stop Ute. But at that point, their mother-daughter relationship had been frail, worn thin by things they both regretted. She wasn't sure that she really wanted to discuss any of this with anyone, but . . . "I'm not sure what I can say, daughter. I worry for his safety. I wish he didn't have to ride ahead. I wish—" But her voice, normally so strong, faltered. She cleared her throat and chuckled. "Well, I wish I could have gone with him."

Rapunzel was a good listener. She made no comment and didn't stir. She simply waited as Katterina gathered her thoughts and tried to swallow the hoarseness out of her voice.

"It's silly to wish such a thing. I suppose it would be inappropriate."

"To be with the man you love?"

Katterina now wound the little thread around her little finger over and over, tighter and tighter. And then she unwound it. And then she wound it again.

"Yes," she breathed out the word at last. She didn't want Rapunzel to say anything. She worried her daughter would say it *was* wrong, that she was awful for loving a monk, that she had no right to love again after making a mess of her own life—making a mess of Rapunzel's life. In truth, she didn't want Rapunzel to judge her.

But her daughter slipped a hand around her shoulder and pulled her close. "I don't know what God has in store, but I'm praying for you. You know, you don't have to feel so alone. I'm here, Paul's here . . . " Her voice drifted away like a petal on the breeze.

A tear slipped down Katterina's face. "Thank you," she said into the darkness.

THE GIANT'S HALL

*E*dmund had to ask, "What is it that I'm missing here?"

"You didn't see her, Your Highness?" The giant gestured to the air.

He shook his head, trying to suppress a scowl.

"There's a woman who appears in these halls. She came here long ago during the War of Sorcery. Amee. She convinced my father's father to join her. My grandmother was a strong woman who stood up to the sorceress and cast my grandfather out for his wicked ways."

Gwynndolen looked intrigued. "How can a wife cast out her own husband?"

"Well, she was the lady. He had only married into the nobility—but more than that, my grandmother was a diffi-cult woman herself, and if she felt you had failed her—that was it."

Edmund made his way back into the conversation. "But that doesn't explain about what you are seeing that I can't see."

"It's part of the curse. Amee comes to check, to see if those here have weakened, are ready at last to join her."

"I'm not sure I understand."

"Amee weighs out who among us might yield and come to her side. She does this throughout all of the Eastern Ports, but usually she does it in such a way that no one can see her."

"So why can the two of you?"

Lord Jalid's thick lips smiled inside his beard again. "Because we are aware."

Edmund felt the scowl return. "Then I should be able to see her."

"Really? You have the mark of one who has touched sorcery yourself."

"Not because he wanted to!" Gwynndolen interceded.

"No, but the stain is there and it encroaches on his soul."

"Who among us has not been stained by the curse of sin? But, with God's help, we do our best, right? His Highness has done no less."

"That may be so, but not all have the gift of discernment, the ability to truly see the shape of the evil coming against, the gift to see how to instead turn to the light so that all things may become new."

"Who among us—"

"You and I can *see*. Perhaps that's why you are here, to help him. To help your kingdom."

Edmund held up a hand. There were more important things to discuss. "But still you haven't explained how we came to be here. How did you help us out of the marsh?"

"Well, that wasn't so hard—you were glazed over in your dehydrated stupor, and even after you had received the proper nourishment, you weren't quite right. But no worries, you seem better after resting all day yesterday."

"All day!" Gwynndolen's eyebrows shot up.

"You needed sleep, so I left you alone."

"Edmund! An entire day gone! How will we get there—"

The giant shook with laughter. "I've said I desire to help you, and so I shall. I have two horses that are yours for the asking. They are specially trained to traverse the swamps and carry you safely to the High King's court. They know the way—you have only to trust them."

Gwynndolen's eyes narrowed, but before Edmund could talk her into accepting the help, the giant spoke.

"I can imagine your feelings, but don't let your pride stop you from reaching the Summer Castle in time. As you know, something has been set in motion, and that fool of a king must be warned—though I would suggest you confide in his wife, if possible. She is the one who truly gets things done there. Now, finish up! You have a couple days' ride ahead of you, but I think you can make it."

A QUESTION OF STRENGTH

*P*aul frowned as the carriages got stuck once more in the spring mud. "We can't pull them out with the horses this tired." He wiped a hand over his face. It was the third time this week they had gotten stuck. Perhaps they should have gone by ship to the High King's castle. Never had it been so important to reach the castle quickly, and never had it been more apparent that even the elements were against them. They had broken an axle and had to find a blacksmith to repair it. They had been stuck in the mud at least twice more. And Helena's fussing never seemed to end. She had been such a happy baby, but now with teething—

At least Jacob and Amis had ridden ahead to warn the Father, but Paul felt something burning within him that said they must hurry, they must be vigilant. He longed to race ahead, but he had a wife and child and mother he must care for. He tried not to think of the adventure he was missing, and he turned his mind instead to think of the safety of those he was to protect. Racing headlong into what could be danger would not be wise.

He frowned, thinking of the wife he wanted to protect.

Rapunzel had barely spoken to him for the last week. Paul knew he had made a mistake, not trusting her with his confidence. She said she would forgive him, but she was no longer open with him.

After a long day of traveling, he sat by the fire next to Dietz. The young man slouched, his mouth slack, his eyes dull. Paul thought of who he had been at that age. Hadn't he been sullen once upon a time when he had had to leave his family for training? And he had not had to witness his family's death. What would the boy—the young man—be thinking? What would be best?

As they finished a quiet meal—how he missed Amis's stories!—he suddenly knew what to do. "Come with me!" he said as he motioned to Dietz.

The boy looked up at him in question. "Where?"

"Just come with me!" Paul selected a few of his best knights and went to the side of the camp, just past where the tents were set up. He handed the boy a staff, much like the one that Jacob had trained him with. Though the staff was not his weapon of choice, he was well-versed with it. Some inner urging told him that it would be a good training weapon for this young man.

First, he reviewed what Jacob had already taught Dietz: how to grip it, how to use the length of it to keep his enemy at bay. With a few strikes, Dietz was sweating, but he beamed at the encouragement he received from Paul. He could do this!

Paul smiled to himself; he had never trained anyone before. He put an arm around the young man's narrow shoulders. "If we train a little every day, you'll get quite adept with the staff by the time we meet up with Jacob, and then he can teach you the more advanced forms."

"Don't you know them yourself?"

Paul laughed. "I know many of them, but I'm not proficient at them. My weapon of choice is a sword. When I'm in a wood, of course, I always bring a bow and arrow, and for the tournament I've trained with a lance and a mace. Each one takes years to master, and I only feel I've just now begun to master the sword."

"You've trained with a mace?" Dietz's voice cracked as he pounced on this information, but Paul kept a straight face as though he hadn't noticed.

"I have. Why?"

"I saw one used in a fight once. Bloody, horrible. It's a vicious weapon." Paul chuckled—he could tell the young man admired the weapon.

"When wielded well, it certainly can be, but it is also easy to manipulate. If your opponent doesn't know what they're doing, you can take advantage of them."

Dietz looked mystified. "How?"

"Each weapon has its own strength and weakness, much like each man does. A staff is strong, blunt, and long. It can keep your enemy farther away so that you can beat them back. But it is dull, so of course it will not cut—and, under the right stress, it can crack and break. The sword can be used to beat, to cut, to pierce, and slay. But it will not bludgeon, and, if forged poorly, will shatter just when you need it most. The bow and arrow are swift, efficient weapons, great at piercing and killing from a distance. At close range, though, they are ineffective. The mace is a bludgeoning tool, and its spikes can kill or harm a man, but two men fighting with them can also get tangled if your enemy is cunning. It takes more time to master the basic form of a mace than a staff and therefore, we begin with the staff."

"Do you complement a man's weaknesses with the advantage of his weapon?"

Paul chuckled. "I hadn't thought of it that way. I suppose that you could, in some ways, but one should concentrate not as much on the weaknesses as the strengths. Finding your strength in combat, speed, strength, and accuracy helps you decide which weapon is yours."

The young man held up a hand. "I've always used a bow and arrow. My brothers wanted me to choose only my fists or magic. But I couldn't. I like to stand far away, quiet. When I see the target—just notch an arrow—let it fly. It's efficient."

"Then you might like the staff the best for hand-to-hand work, though it will bring you in closer contact with your enemy."

"My brothers became my enemies."

Paul was silent for a moment and allowed the sound of their feet slurping the wet ground to fill the air. He noticed the sounds of the birds, the chittering of chipmunks, the scurrying of other woodland creatures as they made their way back to camp. "It is a hard thing when you discover that the ones you should respect and love are opposed to what is good and right."

"I always knew I was different from them. Not just because I was brown, but something inside me told me what we were doing was wrong." Dietz looked away, shoulders rounded again, chin jutted forward.

Paul stopped. "It's not your fault that they chose the wrong way. You are only responsible for your own choices."

"But, when I realized we were wrong, I should have told them. But I just skulked away like a coward." His acidic tone bored into Paul's conscience.

"I'm sorry for that. I'm sorry you didn't feel you had a choice—but you're right, we all have a choice. We also make mistakes, sometimes devastating ones with far-reaching consequences. But that doesn't mean forgiveness is withheld."

"But they can't forgive me. They are lost, for all time. And if I ever meet up with the rest of my family—"

"God, our Maker, can and will forgive you if you just ask with a repentant heart."

"I don't deserve forgiveness."

Paul thought of his father, of all the things he'd wanted to say but had never expressed to the man who had brought about so much harm. He could never fix things between them. The man was lost to him now. "Death is a bitter thing unless we let God have his way in our souls. Don't let it eat at you. Give the burden to him and see how he uses it to make you a better man. Not a one of us deserves forgiveness, and we can never earn it. That's why we need a Savior, don't you think?"

The young man nodded, but it was half-hearted at best. He put a hand on the shoulders that seemed too weak to be carrying this burden. Somehow, they would find their way through. Somehow.

⌒⌒⌒

RAPUNZEL GASPED and sat bolt upright in the tent. Paul startled beside her. "What's wrong?"

"We have to go."

"Go where? What are you—"

"I've seen them—in the marsh. They were captured before they made it to the Father at the monastery. They took them, Paul! They have Jacob and our foolish Amis!"

"Who has them—?" But as he said the words, Paul's face creased in understanding. "Together? Are they together?"

"Yes, Jacob and Amis are—" But he stopped her.

"Not them, the sisters. Amis said they were together—does that mean they have Jacob and Amis with them?"

It was unlike her husband to repeat himself like this. He spoke as he was getting dressed, and she followed suit, grateful that Helena was sleeping soundly, not hearing her.

"They are together. At least I think they are. We need to move swiftly."

"You're not going." Paul's voice lowered, but Rapunzel knew she must. "I have to go—there's something that I must do."

"You must take care of our daughter. That's your job as her mother."

Rapunzel felt as though he had struck her. "We will leave the child with my mother and give instructions for the knights to meet us at the Summer Castle. But we must go now, together. Something in my dream . . . It felt as though God was telling me that I must go. Dietz, too."

"I don't understand—you wanted Helena, and now you would leave her to another's care?"

"Paul! I'm not leaving her, I'm protecting her, just as a mother should. We can't let the sisters of sorcery have their war. There will be no safe place left for our child or for the kingdoms if we don't go now, *together*."

Paul stared at her another moment and then agreed.

THE MARSH

Gwynndolen decided setting off had been easier than carrying on. The deeper they went into the marsh, the harder it became. The horses were well trained and knew which way to go, just as the giant had promised. This road they were following wasn't just a path worn between trees and shrubbery. It had been intentionally created, some sort of rock-and-dirt compilation piled high until it had no longer sunk into the marsh. "We'll have to make certain we check their hooves for rocks each time we stop" was Gwynndolen's only comment as she tried not to let Edmund know how impressed she was.

Edmund didn't seem focused on the threat that was all around. Instead, he gazed around dreamily. She tried to see it as he did, with the heart of a troubadour. The marsh, dark and green, heavy leaves clumped together, swaths of moss trailing down, birds singing, frogs croaking, dragonflies flitting. For a moment, his smile distracted her and she imagined him creating a song about a blue heron, standing in the middle of the waters, lit by a shaft of light breaking through a space between the leaves. Its long, dark beak divided the waters and brought up a fish that it gulped down in a few swallows.

Edmund looked over his shoulder with a whimsical smile. The chirruping of cicadas filled the warm spring air, and the prince almost sang, "Is it me, or should we stop here? There is some bit of magic surrounding this place, isn't there?"

Gwynndolen shook her head. Had he lost his mind? Had she? "Magic? But that's not a good thing."

"Well, perhaps it is God's supernatural handiwork, then. There is something here. We need to stop here in the marsh and—"

"Here in the *swamp*, you mean? This is definitely swamp now. And I do worry about the ground beneath our horse's feet. Perhaps if they had tough pads instead of hooves, then they could traverse the roads and the waters as need be." Her strident tone subtly softened and slowed, again, feeling a tug pull at her. Was it necessary to always be on guard? Perhaps she should relax. "I sometimes wish for a mythical creature of my own, something I could design to have the right kind of feet, the right kind of eyes, ears, nose. It could smell trouble before us, wings to lift us up to the sky if we needed a moment to catch our breath, and then swoop back in for the kill."

Edmund couldn't help laughing. "You're so violent, even in your daydreams."

"I know," she said, then confessed, "Sometimes I fear I'm not the way a proper woman should be at all."

"I don't think that's true. I think you are precisely as you should be. Come, let's stop for a moment. We need to eat something and give the horses a bit of time to rest anyway, don't we?"

Gwynndolen gave him a curious look but stopped her

horse. She dismounted with care not to leave the road that was just wide enough for a narrow carriage. "Should we stop and rest here on the road? It seems strange we haven't seen anyone else, but . . ." Her voice drifted off, pulled away from her thoughts by the call of a whippoorwill in the distance.

Edmund led his horse over to a log, which he touched. Finding it damp, as most things seemed to be, he laid his cloak over it and invited Gwynndolen to sit while the horses lapped up water. Lord Jahid, their kindly giant, had sent them with meat pies whose crusts were sturdy enough to have withstood the last day of travel, but not too tough to bite into. Edmund pulled them out of the knapsack and handed her one. His mouth tipped up and he gestured to a trickle of gravy that escaped the pie and coursed down Gwynndolen's chin. "Not exactly delicate food. I wish I could give you better."

Gwynndolen swiped away the gravy. "As I've said before, Your Highness, I'm not exactly a delicate girl."

He leaned toward her, but then stopped. There was a hush in the swamp; something had happened, some shift, but though they both looked around, they couldn't quite see what it was.

Gwynndolen kept her voice low. "Something's not right here." She stood up, a shimmer right before her catching her eye.

"What is it?"

She shook her head, put down her meat pie, and she took a step forward into rippling waves that didn't feel wet. The prince needed to see what she could see! Glancing behind, she saw Edmund standing next to where she had been sitting, and he looked around, stunned, his meat pie hanging from his hand. "Gwynndolen? Where are you?" His voice sounded far away. He took two steps, and he was at her side.

He tried to reach for her hand but realized he had to shove the remainder of the meat pie in his mouth before he could do so. After struggling to swallow it, he finally managed to ask, "Where are we?"

"I wasn't sure you could follow, since you couldn't see."

"I still can't really see much of anything, just mist all around."

"Yes"—but she began pointing as she spoke, indicating spots—"except here and here and here."

Edmund concentrated on the tip of her finger. "What is it?"

"I don't know, but let's tread carefully."

"Oh, and here I was going to rush about."

She gave him a wry smile. "You would, I suppose."

"Not likely. This is . . ." He paused as he searched for the right word. "This is too odd, too strange."

"Edmund, we need guidance." Her heart thumped and she squeezed his hand.

"You want me to pray?"

"Yes, we need God's help to discern what we've come upon."

Edmund knew she was right, but— "I can't be the one to pray. It needs to be someone pure, someone like you. I'm tainted, I've been the tool of the enemy, the weapon used to bring about death and fear and—"

"God is bigger than her sorcery, he's stronger than their magic. Don't you know this is true? He is ruler of all we see. Ask him to guide you now, and I will follow." She placed her other hand over the top of his hand and closed her eyes.

But Edmund didn't close his eyes. He kept looking around him into the mist. "I can't!" he choked on the words.

Gwynndolen searched his face and then dropped her gaze. "Then I will, but it would be better if the king of Rona did this. I will step in only if I must."

His hand went limp in hers, as though he had failed again. Why didn't he trust that God would listen to his petition, if only he spoke?

Amis looked around him in wonder. What an ingenious way to imprison people! He felt soggy through his entire being; was it probable that he and Jacob would absorb the swamp waters and become bloated? He let his mind tinker with this thought for only a moment. If he contemplated too long, he would descend headfirst into the abyss of lunacy, and he knew that it might not be a long trip for someone of his imaginative inclinations.

"What are you laughing about?" Jacob's stern voice broke through his thoughts, and Amis turned his head a bit to try and speak to the man tied back-to-back with him.

"Was I laughing?"

"Would I have asked what you were laughing about if you weren't, my fool?"

Amis chuckled. "I suppose you wouldn't, my warrior monk."

"Well?"

Amis took a deep breath and thought again about their strangely bloated bodies drifting through the swamps as a warning to others who passed this way. "I'm fairly certain you would not find my thoughts much comfort. I was just thinking—"

"Wait!" The monk's voice cracked.

Amis stopped, a half-smile frozen on his face. He heard an absence in the normal creeping of creatures. There were ripples coming his way. Next to the bulrushes, a redheaded young maid appeared, raising a finger to her lips. The dripping form of the crown prince of Rona rose up behind her, looking just as soggy as Amis felt. He felt a tug on his arms; the binding which constricted his rib cage was pulled, and then it loosened like a vice released.

"Come, let's go before they look for you," the prince said in a forced whisper.

Amis wished he could bow, but if he did, he'd get even wetter. "Thank you for obeying and doing what God wants done to free this land."

Edmund shook his head. "If God could free us, why would he have sent Gwynndolen and me?"

Jacob had naturally taken the lead, finding their way through the reeds. He pulled himself up out of the waters and turned to help the others out. "Because we are commanded to be his hands and feet. The Lord himself will provide a way. He has already given us the blessing—"

"Blessing? All he has done is curse us. If others had not chosen wrongly—if I had not been selfish so many times—even the times I meant for good—"

The girl spoke up from behind the group, the last to receive Jacob's helping hand. "Enough regrets, Edmund. We don't have time for any more. Let's just focus on what's right now, in this moment!"

Jacob reached for an unwieldy branch as though making peace with his limited resources. In the absence of a proper staff, it would have to do. But Amis knew before he could see them that now was the moment of crisis.

The leviathan raised her head from the waters—how long had she been behind them? She transformed to walk on land. "Going so soon, gentlemen? And it seems you have two rescuers. I thought you had given up, little prince. You have no way to control your desires without hurting those you love, but now you've gone into the business of trying to rescue strangers?"

Amis laughed, and pointed to himself with a flourish, despite the gravity of her words. "I am no stranger to the prince. I entertained him last summer."

The maid had taken a defensive stance with her short sword ready to slash at the sorceress. "God sent us here to stop you."

Camilla leaned forward, her pale eyes glowing in the dim light. "And you're supposed to be dead, but instead an entire ship died for you. Why? Because *he* couldn't control his desires."

Amis watched the prince—he hadn't thought a face could get that red! "You're wrong. Her life was worth saving, so I saved it."

"But at what cost? So that you could ruin a kingdom? Or did you think that in saving her, you could still defeat me?"

"We will defeat you!"

"Oh, sister!" She called, and the group looked around for Amee, "Can you hear what they're saying? Do you understand—" But Camilla started, her eyes focused on something they could not see. Her form shimmered, and Amis felt it. He was here.

THE SACRIFICE

It had taken three days of hard riding, but they had found their way to the marsh at last. The farther they went, the quieter Dietz became. When he pulled up on the reins of his horse, Rapunzel rode back to check on the young man before Paul even noticed.

"What is it?"

"My mother—she is near here. This is dangerous." He pulled back on his horse's reins as though to turn away. "I should have never left my family. Never left the Dark Wood. Should have stayed behind with the knights. I'll only cause—"

Rapunzel reached out and touched his arm. "Now is the time we must ride forward and put all other thoughts aside. You have given your life to the one true God and put aside magic. We all have pasts that try to pull us back, but freedom requires us to keep moving forward. Come! Our friends need us!"

CAMILLA SHOOK WITH LAUGHTER, causing Edmund to startle. The leviathan-woman looked over at the centaur who had come out from behind the trees. "You certainly sent him far from you, didn't you, sister? I thought your second child was a girl—that maidservant, Nofra. But she wasn't really yours, was she? She was just a distraction. You had a little boy and sent him away so he wouldn't have to die like his older brother. That must have been when you sent him away— when Eufemia reconnected us to Ute? And I never would have known, had they simply kept him in the Dark Wood."

Amee's huge eyes, more like those of a deer than a horse, filled with unshed tears. "I will give you the girl, but never him."

"I don't need the girl—I need the one you love most."

"I can't lose my last child. Please, not my son."

"It's the only way, sister, it's the only way. Here he comes now, with that little group."

"He is protected—there are many who surround him."

"Not enough to save him from me. How could you be so foolish as to let him come in contact with so many people of the light? That only made him more visible to me. He may bear our mark, but he's pulling away. We must sacrifice him now!"

The tears at last poured out, and her eyes became that of a woman, of a mother begging for the life of her son. "Please, I'll do anything."

"Anything? You are supposed to do *anything* to save our heritage of sorcery from these fearmongers, from these slayers of the dark! Your son wants to be one of them. It would be better for us to curse him and let him die than to let him live and—"

"No!" screamed the mother, rushing at her sister. "I won't let you—"

But Camilla sent her flying backward with a flick of her

tentacle. Amee crashed into a tree trunk, and vines swarmed over her limbs, tying her there.

The centaur crumpled into herself, getting smaller and smaller until she was just a woman, her eyes more human than they had been since she was first possessed of the spirit that allowed her to change forms. Her body heaved with sobs as the vines grew tighter and tighter, pulling her into the rough bark of the tree.

⚬⚬⚬

EDMUND'S HEAD jerked when the warrior monk began to pray in Latin. The words streamed from his lips as he asked the God above to free them, his new staff raised high above his head.

"Stand back!" Camilla's voice raked Edmund's ears as her tentacles reached through the air, one reaching to grab hold of Jacob's staff and another to strangle his neck and cut off his entreaty to his God. Edmund would not—could not let this happen. He could not, if he was going to be who he must be. "Jesu—I wish—I wish to you! Take us and free the land from this curse!" The pain electrified his joints, but he knew he had done the right thing. They would be safe now. He hoped—he trusted it had all been worth it.

The vines retracted their tentacles, releasing their hold on the warrior monk, the fool, and Gwynndolen. A man rushed forward from the shadows, slashing with a sword, crashing into Camilla. But, though the vines had retracted, her tentacles spread up from the waters where she was standing. With one she gripped the hand that held the sword and it splashed into the waters below.

No! Edmund had wished and had prayed. The pain flamed throughout his body. Was he to die and still they wouldn't be free? Camilla laughed, a throaty cackle. "You think it a simple thing? You think all you have to do is make a wish? That's how I get stronger, remember?"

Edmund reached deep within as he looked at the young man. He recognized him. It was the prince that Rapunzel loved. What could save him? What could save them all?

A sacrifice.

A life for a life.

"I pray, Jesu, take my life—it is yours." And a blinding light shot out from him.

THE LIGHT HIT Camilla and she writhed in agony, crumpling into the water. The water, the water, she needed the water. If she could just get deep enough . . . She melted into her leviathan form but didn't have the strength to shoot away. She sank as deep as she could go.

RAPUNZEL FELL face-forward when the light shot through the trees. She and Dietz lay stunned for a moment. When she came to, she was blinded for a moment, and it was all she could to sit up. They slowly gathered themselves and ran the direction that Paul had gone. Why had he left her behind again? He'd asked her to hobble the horses and then left.

Paul was lying on the ground. She ran to him, afraid, but he stirred. She wanted to shake him. "Why did you leave me behind?"

"I'm sorry. I wanted to protect you."

"Then, keep me with you," she cried into his neck. He held her tight, and her anger at all he had not told her washed away. He was alive; that was all that mattered. She was shocked to recognize Edmund, his broken body lying on the ground, a young woman weeping over him. The maid lifted her head—it was Gwynndolen! Nearby, Amis and Jacob were finding their way to their feet.

A crumpled woman bound to a tree reached up and tried to find her way back to standing, struggling out of the vines tying her close. "Who are you?" She looked so frail, so broken beyond repair.

"It's Amee," Jacob answered, "Ute's sister."

"Rapunzel," she whispered, "you lived. Ute didn't kill you?"

"Not for lack of trying. But I survived and saved two of her sacrifices from death."

"You did? Where are they?"

Rapunzel frowned

"Please, I won't hurt them. I just, I want to know if they are—"

"They are well. The girl now belongs to me."

"Keep her safe. A mother should always protect her child."

Rapunzel frowned at the sound of Amee's words. The woman's eyes searched fervently for something behind Rapunzel, so intent that Rapunzel turned to look herself. Out from behind the trees, Dietz emerged, staff in hand like Paul had shown him.

"I knew you'd be safe, my son, I made sure! I kept watch . . ." the woman whispered, giving into her tears again.

"Are you—is she the sorceress?" Clearly, the image he had of the centaur woman was not this trembling mess of tears.

"Yes, I am."

"How can I be your son? How could you send me away?"

"It was the only way I knew to save you."

He stared at his mother as the fool cut the vines from around her. "Should you be setting her free?"

Jacob stepped forward, tying the woman's hands behind her back. "In the name of Jesu, you are bound from using sorcery to hurt us."

"I would never hurt you—you kept my son safe. I don't care what you do with me. Dietz, just remember, I wanted you safe."

The young man took a step toward her, but then turned and walked away.

TALE OF REDEMPTION

Gwynndolen sat on the edge of the bed, her mind spinning. How long did she have to sit here and wait before she could go check on him again? It had taken most of the day and night to reach the High King's Summer Castle, but she hadn't rested her eyes since Edmund fell. She had insisted on being the one to watch over him on the makeshift cot they dragged behind the horses. She kept looking for signs of breathing, praying that God would restore his strength and that he would not be taken from her. Finally, on reaching the castle, she had been sent to her own room with a maid to care for her needs. But in her distress she had pushed the girl out and slammed the door. It had been hours since then, and no one had come to tell her anything.

At last, someone knocked politely on the door. It took all of Gwynndolen's composure not to throw something. "Come in." She forced her voice to stay calm. Perhaps it was someone who could tell her of—

"Gwynndolen?" Rapunzel's voice was sad as she entered with a child on her hip. Gwynndolen began to cry. She didn't even remember the last time she had cried, though she was more accustomed to tears of rage falling down her cheeks, not this weak sadness that left her trembling now. "He's dead, isn't he? You've come to tell me he died."

"What? No! Not at all. Oh, my poor friend, the apothecary has said you can come. He's very weak, but he thinks that Edmund will recover."

Rather than stopping the flow of tears, this made Gwynndolen cry even harder, and Rapunzel came over to her friend and held her while she wept, the little toddler playing at their feet.

⚬⚬⚬

EDMUND LOOKED up and blinked until he could see her face clearly. Why were Gwynndolen's eyes so red? And who were all these people? A swarthy man stood on the opposite side of his sick bed, a massive crown on his head. "We hear you have saved us from an unsavory war."

Edmund tried to speak, but his throat was dry and it took several tries to get the words out. "We certainly tried, Your Majesty. I'm not certain the threat is past." Perhaps if God had accepted his life as a sacrifice—why hadn't he?

The High King nodded like a man who was not used to being gravely serious. "We will discuss things with you tomorrow. You and your companions have had quite an adventure, it seems. One that should make for some good entertainment."

"It's not a song I'd like to sing, Your Majesty."

"That you'd like to—oh, we understand you. Ha ha ha! Wit even while so pale. You Ronans always were good to make us laugh."

Edmund tried to imagine his father ever making any king laugh. No, his imagination failed him. "What I'm trying to say, Your Majesty, is that the threat is not quite extinguished, I'm afraid."

"Is that so?"

"Yes."

"But your friends brought us the sorceress and she is in our dungeons now, even if we can't keep her from changing shapes."

"But there were two of them. The sister—"

"She wouldn't dare to attack us as long as we have her sister in our dungeons. Rest easy, young man. All of the lands beneath our rule are gathering to take counsel. We can celebrate this victory along with my son's birth! You and your friends will have time to tell your tale, but the threat is over. The sisters are separated and, from what we have been told, you deprived Camilla of her power. Not sure that the Father will approve your methods, but we shall wait and see. Now we must see to other pressing matters." And with that, the king left.

"Well, that doesn't bode well," quipped a man wearing a jester's hat at the foot of the bed. This was the fool that he and Gwynndolen had tried to save from Camilla and Amee.

And there was the warrior monk shaking his head. He had the same coloring as the High King, but his dark eyes looked far more intelligent and clear. "I'm afraid you're right, my foolish friend. Are you going to be all right, Your Majesty?" Edmund looked at the other man standing next to the monk who also wore the emblem of the Fisher King's realm. But the warrior monk wasn't speaking to him—he was speaking to Edmund.

"I don't—I'm not the king of Rona. Not yet, anyway."

"The High King will crown you when he crowns me, I suppose." This must be Rapunzel's husband, Prince Paul. "It will all happen after the tournament, I suppose, if there is a tournament. If the sisters truly are defeated."

Rapunzel was watching Edmund closely as he listened to Prince Paul. "I think we should leave you for now, Prince Edmund. There is someone who needs to speak with you."

Gwynndolen stepped forward as the others left his bedside. He stared in disbelief. "Are those tears?"

She flung herself forward and wept on his chest. "I thought you were dead!"

He laughed, but his laughter ended with a moan of pain. "I almost wish I were."

"That's not funny."

"It is, a little."

"You sacrificed yourself—"

"Not well enough, God didn't take me, and Camilla got away."

"You are a fool. Don't you see? You are God's man now. He accepted you. And I'm not worried about Camilla, God's not done yet."

He reached up and brushed a tear from her lashes. "You don't think so?"

"No, I think he is still at work. Which is good, because that king is a fool and might get us all—"

But Edmund didn't wait to hear what she was going to say next. He pulled her closer and she stopped talking. "Are you trying to kiss me? Now?"

He answered in the only way he could.

WANT MORE NOW?

What greed set Rapunzel's destiny in motion?

Eufemia and Katterina have always been close. Cloistered in their small home and selling cheese at the market while their mother lies sick is the only life they've known. But when Eufemia is cursed by an old woman, something twists inside her. She will never be the same.

Before the sisters lie two paths on life's journey. Katterina discovers she can have a family of her own, but only if she denies Eufemia of the man they both want. Eufemia, apprenticed up in a cove in the Soontrisse Mountains to an old widow whose health is failing, realizes the woman is not what she seems. Katterina grows suspicious; what is Eufemia really learning?

One curse. Two secrets. Betrayal in the garden will lead to Rapunzel's tower.

Receive your copy of *Before the Tower* by visiting
dl.bookfunnel.com/wftepfzx96

I SHARE monthly book updates and recommendations from my reading life at authorjroe.com/category/books-worth-reading. I look forward to connecting with you and hearing what YA fantasy books you are loving.

IF YOU ENJOYED Under the Curse, please take a moment and leave a review on the retailer where you purchased it and over on Goodreads. Thank you for helping other wonderful readers like you find this series!

TURN THE PAGE FOR A SNEAK PEEK OF
AMONG THE KINGDOMS,
COMING 2021!

authorjroe.com/book/among-the-kingdoms

Camilla had been waiting. She'd been listening. It had taken time to locate another source of power she could manipulate, but at last she had found the young maid. Deep in the swamps, she had collected again what little strength she could summon. She would need to go out to deeper waters soon. But not yet.

Nofra was sitting on a mossy log, silent tears wandering down her lovely brown face. Her curly dark hair, braided to the side, was resting over her shoulder. Her dark eyes were unfocused. Unaware of the patchy light straining through the dim trees. Unaware of the sorceress as she rose to the surface. Camilla's sleek, eel-like body morphed into a towering woman whose auburn hair streamed water. The maid turned and stared at the sorceress.

"You know who I am?"

Nofra nodded, mouth agape.

"You were sworn to my sister, and she used you—but I will never use you like that. You will be my vessel and I will grant you power, as long as you bind yourself to me. Do you understand? Only me, never to Amee again—or any other," she added.

The girl nodded, ringlets at the tail of her braid bobbing.

"You will be more powerful than you can fathom. Just imagine, together we will make the kingdoms crumble. You want to be a queen? You can be. You want to be a sorceress? You will be! But you must be mine. At all costs."

The maid's dark eyes filled. "Will I never see my mother again?"

Camilla's voice thundered, and the maid shrunk into herself. "You call her that? After how she abandoned you? She betrayed you, betrayed us all! How can you—" She broke off when the maid lifted a tentative hand.

"But she's all I've ever known."

"Until now." Camilla's lips split into a sneer. "Come, let's gather our people together. It's time for war."

GLOSSARY

Chemise — a slip-like gown that was worn as the first layer of dress for women in Rapunzel's world. It would be naturally colored, typically an off-white color. Often, this was worn as a nightgown at night when the other layers of dress would be removed.

Cotehardie — a fitted gown worn over the chemise with sleeves cut to various lengths according to station in Rapunzel's world. The higher the station, the more intricate the sleeves, sometimes tight at the elbows and bell-shaped at the wrist or short at the elbows with a streaming tail called a tippet. The bottom of the cotehardie might also be lined with fur to show off the station of a woman.

Coven — in Rapunzel's world, this is a grouping of warlocks and witches that gather in secret to practice the dark arts to return their world back to an acceptance of sorcery.

Hosen — leggings worn to protect the legs.

Sorcereress/Sorcerer — a female or male who has achieved a master status in the practice of the dark arts of magic.

Surcoat — the outermost layer of dress a woman would wear in Rapunzel's world, over which she would wear a cloak to go outdoors in cool weather. The gown was sideless and would complement the cotehardie's coloring, often cut a bit short if the cotehardie beneath had a fur-lined hem. The surcoat was frequently embellished with embroidery.

Tippet — long, streaming tails extending from the elbows of a woman's cotehardie sleeves, denoting a high station in society. Common throughout the High King's lands.

AUTHOR'S NOTE AND THE JOURNEY

Not that long ago, I discovered that the word for "curse" was the same as the word for "blessing" in the Hebrew language. I wondered, how could the reader know which one the author meant? Turns out, it's all in the context.

At the end of the first three books, I ended with several questions to explore your own journey with some of the questions that Rapunzel and her friends were working through. This time, I just want to share some of what was in my heart as I wrote this particular book.

You may have noticed that this road keeps leading to a similar theme. In fact, it may be a question you have asked yourself:

Why does God allow horrible things to happen?

In my own life, I have gone through traumatic hardships. Days before Beyond the Tower was published, my brain-injured sister, for whom I was a caregiver, was run over by a truck while she was sleeping. You may have to go back and reread that particular sentence again. How does someone get run over while they are safely asleep in bed? It shouldn't happen. How could a good God let something that horrible happen to someone who was already vulnerable? This wasn't the first awful thing God had allowed in my life, I've struggled with chronic illness and severe depression since high school. Losing my sister sent me back to those dark times.

I knew all the "right" answers to all the hard questions. I'm a pastor's wife and I went to Bible college, so I should be able to weather the storm, right?

But like Rapunzel, like Edmund, I couldn't understand God's plan. Where was his hand when things were so twisted and wrong? My life felt like a curse, and though I had wonderful people I loved, I gave into despair and found myself contemplating suicide.

But God connected me to an amazing grief counselor who helped me recognize the beauty inherent in the life he has given me. Even a life without the sister I adored and whom I thought I would be taking care of for the rest of my life.

In Romans chapter 8, verses 26-28, I found great comfort. The image of the Spirit of God interceding to God the Father for me with his own groanings when I didn't have words to express my grief, my despair, or my fears meant everything. And to know that nothing could separate me from God's love was another truth that broke through my depression. It broke through the lie that my life was worthless. Because God the Father would not have sent his one and only Son to die for me if I was worthless.

Like Rapunzel, Edmund doesn't know what to do with this truth. What kind of life will God have for him, now that he has given it to God? What kind of man, what kind of king will he be? And as Rapunzel and Katterina try to be the mothers they want to be, how will their relationship shape them?

I don't know exactly what's going to happen in my own life next, but I'm no longer living in fear. I've left that tower behind. Like my friends in these pages, I want the curse that once bound me to sin to now be a blessing to others. I can see how easily my life could have been useful for nothing and no one, but God saved me from that. He saved me for loving him and loving others.

What is around the next corner? Probably more misadventures, some hilarious (thank you, Amis) and some very hard. Whatever comes, though, we have a God who fights for us and loves us. I hope that you know that. It is my prayer.

See you when The Journey resumes.

Who shall separate us from the love of Christ? Shall tribulation, or distress, or persecution, or famine, or nakedness, or danger, or sword? As it is written,

"For your sake we are being killed all the day long;
we are regarded as sheep to be slaughtered."

No, in all these things we are more than conquerors through him who loved us. For I am sure that neither death nor life, nor angels nor rulers, nor things present nor things to come, nor powers, nor height nor depth, nor anything else in all creation, will be able to separate us from the love of God in Christ Jesus our Lord. (Romans 8:35-39)

ACKNOWLEDGMENTS

As always, there are so many to thank, and the deadline for this book looms. I will keep it short this time. To my husband, Jeff, for believing my strange stories could make a difference, I'll always be grateful. Katie, Sydney, and Caleb, I am forever thankful for your enthusiasm and your love. Joy, Jeanine, and Jessica, you have forever shaped me. Dad and Mom, thank you for raising me! To Margaret, Alison, and Lora--I love you! Uncle Doug, Aunt Celia, you are truly the best. Heather, Mike, Josh, Travis, and Sean, it is a blast to be a book nerd with all of you. Colin, Tamami, Eris, and Zen, I am loving getting to know you better, and I'm so happy Eris can share her art expertise with my covers.

Jody, you are more than an editor or typesetter. You are the best friend and sister I didn't know I needed! To my sisters of the heart (and one brother), Lauren, Heather, and Kevin, I praise God for your friendship and laughter that has spanned decades now. And to the gaggle of children we are raising--I love how they love each other! Emory, Sophie, Phoebe, Harrison, and Ethan; you rock! Bob, Margie, Rachel, and Kelly, your prayers and love have sustained me.

Justin, Sarah, and Eva, I love you three. Gwynn, you are the prayer warrior that kept me going. I miss you more than I can say.

To the Weekend Writing Warriors, I'm so glad we are on this journey together. And lastly, with a debt I cannot repay, thank you to my betas: Sydney, Allison, Mary, and Bree. Thank you for caring for these words, helping them uplift and never harm in these confusing times.

ABOUT THE AUTHOR

A lover of books and fairytales, JacQueline uses her faith and life experience with chronic pain/depression to discover new ways of telling old stories as well as her own. She lives in North Alabama with her amazing karate husband and three book-crazy children. She takes every opportunity to drink coffee while wearing dangly earrings and the color purple. Join her newsletter when you download your free copy of *Before the Tower* by visiting dl.bookfunnel.com/wftepfzx96.

Find JacQueline at AuthorJRoe.com, and you can also follow her on social media:

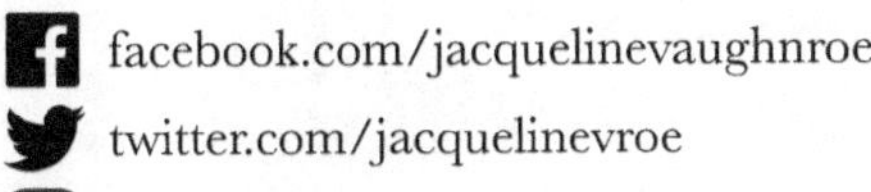

facebook.com/jacquelinevaughnroe

twitter.com/jacquelinevroe

instagram.com/jacquelinevaughnroe

www.ingramcontent.com/pod-product-compliance
Lightning Source LLC
Chambersburg PA
CBHW061601190726
48288CB00007B/2126